PEOPLE

—OF THE—

NIGHT

J. LINDSEY WILLIS

ISBN: 978-1-63950-175-5 (sc)
ISBN: 978-1-63950-176-2 (e)

Writers Apex

Gateway Towards Success

8063 MADISON AVE #1252
Indianapolis, IN 46227
+13176596889
www.writersapex.com

M an, how did I end up in this situation? It just seems like yesterday that I was sitting at John's house. I couldn't stand listening to him ramble about how he was about to score thirty points in our game against Battlefield College. Now John was lucky if he were going to play thirty minutes for the whole game!

The only reason John is on the team is the head coach is his godfather. Coach Kelly gets on my nerves with his want-to-be Coach Carter ways. Do not get me wrong; Coach Kelly is good at what he does, but I think he could be a little bit anal sometimes. They are both suckers.

I guess that is not important right now since I am five hours away from campus. The worst part of this situation is I have no way of getting back to campus before curfew. What was I thinking about messing with this chick? The things I get myself into sometimes make me wonder why I am still here. Man, this chick almost cost me to lose everything that I love.

I should have known something was up when she kept asking about when daylight saving time is. But being my typical self, I thought I could charm her out of her draws and some money to get me through the weekend. The USCAA doesn't believe in letting ballplayers correction student athletes to have extra. So until I get to the GBA, I got to get in where I fit in.

Oh, I'm sorry for being rude. My name is Derrick Arthur, but everybody in the D'Ville knows me as DA.

Now this chick was supposed to go the hotel, away from campus, you see. So we could get our nightlife and dung dragon on. A brother has to keep a low profile, especially when you are the breadwinner for

D'Ville St. One more year from now, I will be living large and in charge in the GBA.

Now while this chick was snorting too much of that nightlife at one time, something or someone told me to get up and leave. Then I called up my man Spiff and told him to meet me at the Wayside Hotel. Now I knew Spiff was going to give me a long speech about my movements, but I also knew that no matter what, I could always count on Spiff to have my back and get out of these tight situations.

"Come on, DA! What is going through that head of your, man? Smoking Dung Dragons with a night crawler? Are you trying to throw away what the undisputed master J. Boogie has blessed you with?"

I told you he was going to lecture me all the way back to campus. Spiff is cool, and I know he means well, but he is always coming at me every chance he gets with this day walker, night crawler stuff. I just think people are going to do whatever they want to do whether the sun is up or down.

Does the sun and moon really play a part on how people act? I'm just saying! Maybe I'll find out the answer one day. Man, I must be high to even let my mind contemplate this! I want to tell Spiff about the strange voice that told me to leave, but I'm not in the mood for him to get all spiritual on me! I'll just take a shower, call Shavon, and then pass out! Got practice in the morning.

CHAPTER

1

It was 5:00 a.m. when Derrick's alarm clock went off. Derrick had half an hour to get dressed and make it to practice.

"Man, I can't afford to be late to practice this morning! This is one time I prefer not to run wind sprints until I puke!" Coach Kelly was one of those militant type of guys who believe in discipline and not excuses. "I believe Coach needs some pregame sex to calm down his power trip!" Derrick said to himself.

Derrick remembered that he was supposed to call Shavon last night. "I will call her when I get out of class at 9:00 a.m." Shavon doesn't have her creative writing class until 11:30 a.m. So that gave him enough time to practice, shower, get some breakfast, and get a quick nap.

Derrick couldn't stop thinking about what Spiff was saying about that day walker, night crawler stuff. "I'm no different from the next individual out here! OK, maybe I could do some things a little different, but like I said, I'm *just like everybody else!*"

Derrick noticed that he was the first one in the locker room. He figured it couldn't hurt to shoot some jump shots before the rest of the team gets to practice. While he was shooting jump shots, Spiff and Brad had entered the gym.

"Hey, DA! Stop trying to be like John!" Brad said.

"Yeah, Derrick. You could shoot three hundred jumpers, and you still would not be a good shooter!" Spiff stated.

"We all know how John made this team!" Derrick shouted back.

"Stop hating on John D. You and everybody knows that his jump shot is automatic like Jesus in *He Got Game*." Spiff responded. Derrick knew deep down Spiff and Brad were right, but he could not come to grips with the fact that a dude like Goldstein, who was accepted to IQ College, decides to take a handout from his godfather coach and rob a brother who actually needed a full ride on the team so he can have an opportunity to make of something of himself.

I guess Derrick was angry that John came from publicity and didn't need basketball to get a quality education, and he did. It was just amazing how this system would bring individuals from different levels of life just to serve a common goal.

Coach Kelly walked in the gym and then blew his whistle to get the team's attention. He gave this speech about the importance of character and smart decision making! He then blew his whistle a second time, had the team play a scrimmage, shot one hundred free throws, and ran twenty wind sprints to get ready for their game against Battlefield College.

Now it was 8:56 a.m. Derrick felt that it was the right time to call Shavon. Just before Derrick opened up his phone, he just thought about how special she was to him. Shavon is the total package. She is a real Nubian Queen, very down to earth, has an inner beauty that radiates to her outer core! She is a well-coordinated woman who sees beauty in the darkest situations; plus, she always see right through Derrick when he tries to BS her. She is always cool and calm, which frightens Derrick sometimes. Now let's listen in to Derrick's phone call.

"Hey, Shavon, my sexy butterfly. I missed you today, beautiful! I was thinking about you all morning, even at practice, baby!"

"The only thing you missed today at practice was your jump shots, Derrick!"

"Just teasing, baby. So is everything OK?"

Derrick wanted to tell Shavon about the conversation he had with Spiff, his personal hang-up with John Goldstein, and how he felt Coach

Kelly plays favorites with certain players. But being the typical male who is taught to never show your emotions, Derrick just played it off and said, "I'm straight, baby! You know who you're talking to? You're talking to DA, better known as *da man with da master plan!*"

"Derrick, now you know every time you refer to your alter ego, something is bothering you! This is your baby Shavon *you are talking to,* and, baby, you don't have to be macho for me!"

"I told you, readers, Shavon sees right through me, like that chick in the movie *Why Did I Get Married?* That's why I love her."

"OK, Von–Von, I need your presence so I can tell you what is on my brain."

"Derrick, I will see you later. Got to get ready for class, and I will definitely hold my baby and nurse his wounds! Work on your jump shot and study for your intro to *The Good Book* midterm! *Bye,* DA," Shavon said sarcastically.

"Talk to you later, sexy butterfly!" Derrick said in a smooth, deep voice, trying to sound like the father of love Larry Black.

———————

CHAPTER

2

———————

It was 12:57 p.m., and Brad decided to take a ride into town with the Goldsteins. John and Brad had been friends ever since John's freshman year at D'Ville St. Now John was what you called a privileged child. His father Stan Goldstein is an alumni and big-time booster to D'Ville St. John always talked about how his father pretty much owns D'Ville and how he has everyone in his back pocket.

Stan stated, "As long as we have bottom feeders, I will always have *money!*" Stan Goldstein owns the biggest law firm in D'Ville, Good As Gold Law Firm. As for John's mother, she's a stay-at-home housewife who loves *the power and prestige* of being Mrs. Stan Goldstein.

Now Brad could not understand why Derrick did not like John. Brad felt that John was a cool guy. John invited the whole team over to his house just to show he wasn't some stuck-up spoiled rich kid who thought he was better than everyone else.

As Stan drove past Club Blackout, he asked his son and Brad what they see. John and Brad both looked at each other with a puzzled look. Then John said, "We see a club, Dad."

"No, son. What you see is profit! When Foolish Friday rolls around, every *bottom feeder, night crawler,* so-called day walker, and man or woman of elevation is going to be *begging me to keep them from being sent to B-Have County!*"

When Stan finished his statement, he took a puff from his cigar, blew the smoke in the air, and said how this year was going to be a great year for Good as Gold Law Firm.

Now John shared most of his father's views about life but had some differences about his father's philosophy about *power*. When Stan drove up to their house, he looked at John and Brad and then got out of his car, as he knew they were up to something. When John and Brad got out of the car, John began to explain to Brad that he had been studying from this new book.

Brad thought John was talking about a book from their biology 305 class, but when John showed Brad the book, Brad had a bad feeling John was way over his head. John saw this newfound fear that was written all over Brad's face. John told him that this book was scientific as well as spiritual. He also stated how he went to some of the meetings to get a better understanding of how people make their movements. As Brad was about to leave, John gave him the information on where he can order the book, plus the time and address to the next meeting.

In the world below, MD 20/20 was getting ready to put his evil plan into play. "It's almost time to wreak *havoc on the people! First, D'Ville. Then the rest of the world!*" As soon as MD 20/20 finished his statement, Shadow No. 1 and Shadow No. 5 came in with their annual *havoc report.*

"Shadow No. 1, what do you have for me?" asked MD 20/20. Shadow No. 1 stated how he was about to put the finishing touches on getting the Super Galaxy Wrestling Champion Leaping Lenny Wilson to give up his ultimate being. "That's it? That's all you got?" stated MD 20/20.

All the other 1shadows began laughing hysterically. MD 20/20 started to spit fire at Shadow Nos. 7, 9, 10, and 12 to 20. The rest of shadows started trembling with fear. Then MD 20/20 grabbed Shadow No. 1 by his throat and opened up the dungeon of light. All Shadow No. 1 could do was hope another shadow would do something, anything to take the heat off him.

MD 20/20 asked Shadow No. 1, "Why shouldn't I throw you in this dungeon, you stupid shadow? Answer me, fool!" Shadow No. 1 had to think of something quick, so he lied and said it was Shadow No. 8's plan to go after Leaping Lenny Wilson instead of staying with Andy Schwartz. MD 20/20 threw Shadow No. 1 down to the ground and then picked up Shadow No. 8. He clipped his wings and threw him in the *pit of beasts.*

MD 20/20 turned around and said that Leaping Lenny Wilson was not a threat to their kingdom or their plan. All the shadows were speechless, knowing how unmerciful their master is, especially when he loses an ultimate being to J. Boogie. MD 20/20 loves hearing the so-called people's ultimate beings scream in horror as he terrifies them in his world below.

MD 20/20 told his shadows that if they want to be in *the circle of darkness,* they will do whatever they got to do to please him and see that his kingdom destroys the other kingdom.

There was a catch to MD 20/20's evil plan. It was *the golden rule of balance.* MD 20/20 and his shadows could only leave the world below when it was dark. MD 20/20 wanted total control of *the universe,* but he needed twelve months of total darkness in order to accomplish this.

As Derrick began making his way to Shavon's dorm, he began to feel a strange and unusual presence around him. He stopped and observed his surroundings. Then he realized that nothing unusual was going on—just students walking around campus looking to enjoy these last couple of days of *daylight.*

As Derrick continued to walk to Shavon's dorm, a couple of females wished Derrick good luck against Battle Field College on Friday. Derrick responded by saying that he didn't need luck. He was blessed with skills, and he will lead D'Ville St. to the *promised land.* Then the females smiled and said in a seductive voice, "We want to take you to the promised land, champ!" Derrick just laughed it off and continued on his merry way to Shavon.

Just before he reached her room, his cell phone began to ring. Derrick started not to answer it but saw that it was his friend and teammate Smoove. "What's happening, DA?"

"Hey, Nathan!" Derrick said sarcastically.

"Come on, Derrick. Stop calling me by my government!" Smoove shouted back. "You know I'm the Smoovest dude in D'Ville!"

Now Derrick had to admit Nathan Rodgers could talk his way out of anything. To Derrick, it seemed that everything in life just went Smoove for Nathan—from the way he plays basketball to his relationships with people. Even getting straight *A's* came naturally to him. *Some guys just have all the luck!* Derrick thought to himself.

"Hello, Earth to Derrick. Can you hear me now? Can you hear me now?" Derrick snapped out of his thoughts and answered, "Yeah, Smoove. I'm here. Sorry about that. Must have lost signal."

"That's OK, buddy. I just called to find out if you wanted to go to Club Blackout on Friday after the game."

Derrick knew that this Friday night is Foolish Friday, and when the clock strikes midnight, everyone is going to act a fool because of the first of a nine-month period of darkness.

Derrick told Smoove he would let him know after the game. Then he said to Smoove in a sarcastic voice, "I hope your game against Battle Field College is Smoove, so we could get this booster money!"

Smoove stated, "Man, Battle Field College Alumni is going to have to pay me to stop making these *silky Smoove passes* against their weak two-three zone. Plus, you know we going to run them out of the gym as long as you don't shoot that weak jumper!" Derrick laughed off Smoove's last comment, and then they both hung up.

As Derrick approached Shavon's door, he noticed the sound of an electric guitar and knew that Shavon's cousin must have come to visit for the weekend. When Shavon opened the door and welcomed Derrick with a kiss, he looked over to his left and saw Amy listening to her favorite heavy metal group Civilian SledgeHammer.

"Hey, DA," Amy said from the living room. "I hope you treating my cousin right because if you're not, I'm going to have to bust you up Leaping Lenny Wilson style!"

"Please, Amy! You don't want to feel the wrath of *the most explosive man in the universe!*" Derrick replied as he began to flex his muscles.

Then Shavon came into the living room, watching Derrick and Amy imitate their favorite wrestlers. "Amy, I know you don't think Leaping Lenny Wilson stands a chance against Geronimo Jones?" Derrick asked.

"Of course, I do, Derrick! He is *the greatest,* and *he is sooooo cute!*" Derrick looked at Shavon and thought Amy was crazy. Then he shook his head and remembered that Amy was into the rock-and-roll, stuntman type. Then Derrick said, "Well, I guess any female who listens to Civilian SledgeHammer would think that Leaping Lenny Wilson is *sooooo cute!*" Both Derrick and Amy laughed, and Amy said that Derrick made a great point. Derrick said goodbye to Amy and followed Shavon into her bedroom.

As Derrick and Shavon entered her bedroom, Derrick just plopped down on her bed, looked up at the ceiling, and began to think about all the things Spiff said to him the night before and how strange it is going to be to all of a sudden go through the next nine months of no daylight. This had been going on in D'Ville for a while, but for some strange reason, Derrick felt something out of the ordinary was about to happen. But he couldn't make any sense of it.

Shavon lay down next to Derrick and asked him to let it all out. "Sweetheart, you can relax and tell me what is on your mind as well as your heart! I'm here for you, and *I love you,* Derrick, or should I say DA! Ha-ha-ha!"

"OK, Von-Von. How could I explain this? I feel like something or someone is trying to get my *attention!* I was in a situation, and something on the inside told me to get away because *danger* was lurking around the corner. I listened to that voice, and sure enough, someone tried to rob D'Ville National Bank as I was about to go and make a deposit."

Instead, Derrick decided to go to John's house with Spiff, Brad, and Smoove. When they got over to John's house, Derrick noticed that the same bank he was about to go to was on the six o'clock news. Two people was wounded in the bank robbery. Even though that happened a week ago, Derrick was still bothered by it. Derrick couldn't make sense of this illogical world he was living in. *It was really starting to get to him.*

Shavon just watched the love of her life's eyes fill up with water as he continued to express himself. She also knew there was something else bothering him, but she didn't want Derrick to hold anything back if she probed him with what he called her a million and one questions. Then Derrick asked Shavon, "Baby, did you ever feel like you were chosen to do something but don't know what you were chosen for?"

Shavon began to smile and kissed Derrick with a lot of passion. Shavon always knew deep down that there was something very special about Derrick, and she felt it in her ultimate being. She also wished that Derrick would continue to listen to his ultimate being.

Then Derrick pulled Shavon away so he could look into her beautiful catlike eyes and let the sounds of Larry Black take them to *the palace of love.*

3

On the south wing of campus, Brad was walking to the address John had given him the other day. Brad didn't get caught up with the theories of why this or why that. He was open to *anyone's way of thinking*. He believed everyone could get along regardless of their differences.

As Brad approached the building, he paused, looked at the address again, and then realized the unique structure of the building. The building was at least fifty stories high, but it looked like it formed a backward number seven. Then Brad noticed John standing in the lobby talking with some older guys.

When Brad walked in, he felt this strong sensation flowing through his body. And without even looking in Brad's direction, John said, "Hey, Brad. Thanks for letting your presence be known!" Now Brad was curious how John knew he had entered the building. Then Brad said to himself, "John was at least twenty-five feet away engaged in a deep conversation with those other guys! I guess there is some truth to the principles of this book called *The Strategy*."

"There is more truth than you could ever imagine!" John answered. That is when Brad realized how John was able to read and answer his thoughts by feeling Brad's sequences of movement. Then Brad thought about the first chapter he read. It was called "The First Move."

The closer Brad approached John, the clearer Brad was able to listen to John talk to him through his mind while he was talking out loud to the four other guys. When John finished talking to the four guys, he faced Brad, gave him a half smile, and said, "Movement tells all, *but if you stand still, then someone else can move you!*" Brad could see this new look in John's eyes, almost as if someone or something gave him this new aura of *invincibility*. Brad was more curious about this new feeling of *power*. That sensation he felt grew stronger and *stronger. Brad loved this feeling.* page 10.

Derrick looked at the clock and noticed that at midnight, the sun would have set for the next nine months. He just lay there in a trance, wondering what is in store for Foolish Friday. Just as he was about to get up, Shavon pulled him back down and gave him a passionate kiss. She then encouraged him to play his game and to not worry about the outcome.

Derrick embraced her sweet lips and encouraging words that had him feeling like a million bucks. Shavon pulled the covers over her face as Derrick pushed back the curtains. She knew how much Derrick enjoyed *watching the sunrise,* especially on game day. As Derrick was taking in the rays, his phone started ringing, and he saw it was Spiff.

"Hey, DA. Sorry for calling you this early, but I just finished having a conversation with *the master.*"

"Come on, Spiff! It's too early for you to get all *spiritual* on me right now! I'm trying to get my mind right for tonight!" Derrick interrupted.

Then Spiff said in a sarcastic voice, "Tell Shavon I said to let you talk, or do you have to run her bathwater and make her breakfast?" Derrick told Shavon what Spiff had said, and all three of them began to laugh. Now Spiff went on to explain how he had this feeling that something strange was looming. Spiff also felt a newfound evil that was making its way to D'Ville.

As Derrick continued to listen to Spiff, he began to wonder, *Was it all a coincidence, or was it all part of some mystical plan?* This was beginning to get kind of spooky to Derrick. The last time he felt like this was when Spiff picked him up from the hotel the other night.

"So, DA, you and Shavon want to go come with me to the *day walker rival?* We could go after the game tonight!" Spiff stated. Derrick was hesitant to accept Spiff's invitation. He knew Spiff meant well, but he didn't want to get into all of that *"people of the night" stuff.*

Derrick planed on going to D'Ville Square to watch the *sunset.* It was a tradition he started five years ago. Plus, Derrick had other things in mind, like smoking a Dungeon Dragon or two and get totally wasted celebrating his championship drinking Hyenna Lagers.

"Remember, DA, *you owe me.* Plus, I told you the Master of The Universe wants you to become one with your ultimate being!" Derrick knew that deep down in his ultimate being that Spiff was right. Then he thought about his conversation with Shavon and agreed to go with him.

Now *in* the skies above, the Master of The Universe has informed J. Boogie to have all of the GL's (guiding lights) to meet in Area 21. All the GL's knew that they only meet in Area 21 when it is time to prepare for the battle of *destiny.* As the horn played, a new GL was earning his top flight and receiving his assignment.

After the ceremony, J. Boogie entered Area 21 with the following words of wisdom: "My fellow warriors, the day has come when MD 20/20 and his shadows of 3D will come and try to make, as many believe, that darkness is the new light. We must keep a close eye on their evildoings. I want six GL's protecting Leaping Lenny Wilson at all times. I don't know how much longer he could withhold Shadow No. 1's attacks. GL's 1 through 6 accepted their mission, gave J. Boogie a hug of victory, then they was off to protect Leaping Lenny Wilson."

Then the new GL had entered Area 21. J. Boogie gave him the name GL 53. GL 53 was given special instructions on how to stay focused on his assignment. J. Boogie explained how the battle between MD 20/20 and his shadows is fierce, and some GL's have been tricked into following him. Plus, J. Boogie also explained to GL 53 that might have to sacrifice his top flight if it means bringing an individual to become one with the undisputed Master of The Universe.

GL 53 took in J. Boogie's words of wisdom. Then he promised J. Boogie that he will do *whatever it takes to accomplish his assignment and bring victory to the skies above.*

CHAPTER

4

The moment of truth has finally come. The USCAA Championship against Battle Field College has arrived. Coach Kelly was looking over his game plan for the tenth time in the past hour. This game was the biggest he had ever coached in, so he wanted to be prepared.

Coach was thinking about starting John at shooting guard and Derrick at small forward. Coach knew that Spiff would not mind being taken out of the starting lineup if it meant helping the team win. It was Derrick that had Coach nervous about using this lineup.

Everyone on the team knew that Derrick and John would make the perfect one, two punch like Mike and Scottie of the good old days. *With Derrick driving to the basket at will and John's impressive sharpshooting, Battle Field College would not what hit them!* Coach thought to himself. Everyone on the team also knew that Derrick did not get along with John for whatever reason, and Derrick always felt that he had to prove he was better.

Coach Kelly knew deep down in his ultimate being that he had to start John because he gave them an advantage every time he was on the court. Coach thought to himself how John always seemed to always be at the right place at the right time. John seemed to always give D'Ville that extra ump when he came off the bench. John's clutch shooting in the semifinal and his last-second steal gave D'Ville the victory.

Coach Kelly also knew the last-second change would throw Battle Field College off. The phone inside the locker room began to ring. When Coach Kelly saw what number appeared on the caller ID, he just took a deep breath and braced himself for the unwanted conversation.

"Hey, Coach. I just wanted to wish you good luck tonight! I got a lot of faith in your team to pull it out!" Coach Kelly's body tensed up when this deep, mysterious voice said he had a lot of faith in his team. Coach Kelly knew this person only believed in *wealth* and *power*.

Then he let Coach know who he felt should start with Nathan, Brad, and Derrick. That's when Coach knew that John was going to start over Spiff whether Derrick liked it or not. Then the mysterious voice stated, "Coach, your future is getting *bright,* but if you make me *lose my faith in you,* then every day will feel like a Foolish Friday. If you know what I mean! But I know you will get the job done!" Then Coach heard the dial tone.

Coach was so nervous after the phone conversation he went to his private bathroom to splash some water on his face. But his launch decided to make an early exit. Coach couldn't stop shaking, so he went into his travel bag and pulled out a bottle of his favorite wine called Redemption. He poured himself a cup and took his calm medicine to bring him back to a relax state of mind. Then Coach took a shower, got dressed, and was ready to address his team with their assignments to bring victory over Battle Field College.

The team was sitting in the locker room waiting on Coach Kelly. Spiff approached Derrick to explain to him how he felt something was going to change. On the other side of the locker room, Brad and John were having their own conversation. And it had nothing to do with basketball.

"Hey, John. I just want to say thanks for inviting me to—"

"Don't mention it!" John stated before Brad could finish. John went on to explain how things were going to get real foolish as he put his plan into play. Brad tried to read John's mind to understand what his plan was just to be interrupted by Spiff, Smoove, and Derrick.

When Brad noticed Spiff, Smoove, and Derrick standing at his locker, he stared at them like they were going to attack him. "Hello,

Earth to Brad? Hey, can you hear me now?" Smoove said. Then Brad woke up out of a trance. John just used chapter 7 of *The Strategy* to feel Derrick's inner thoughts through Brad.

John knew Derrick was smart and could see things from a deep perspective. John also knew that Derrick's anger gets in the way of his super vision. If there is anyone who could expose him of his false sense of power, it is Derrick.

Even though Spiff was a day walker, John did not see Spiff as a threat. Yes, it is true that day walkers always focus on the dawn of the new day, but some people say they fear those who use *The Strategy.* According to the great strategist, day walkers feel that science is evil, and the Master of The Universe is an artist. The great strategist also said that day walkers fail to realize that the Master of The Universe created MD 20/20 to bring darkness into the world.

John flashed a smile at Brad as he watched Spiff, Smoove, and Derrick try to have a conversation with him. Then Brad realized what John was doing. Brad looked at Spiff and then Smoove and then Derrick. He began to hear a collection of voices, and all types of thoughts flooded his mind.

Brad thought back to that night at the meeting. Brad now knew that he was just a pawn in John's plan. Brad began to feel very uneasy knowing John had access to his mind. It scared him, but he knew that he could not give into the fear according to chapter 2.1 of *The Strategy.*

The D'Ville Arena was packed. Everybody from alumni to the regular locals was there. Everything was going good until Coach sprung that last-second line up change.

"What was Coach trying to imply? That Derrick DA Man Arthur cannot lead us to the promised land? Man, this Goldstein dude is getting on my last nerve! I'm not going to be rebellious."

Derrick's plan was to play within the system, get his stock up for the GBA draft, and leave D'Ville for good. Derrick made up his mind that he could not take another year of playing under Coach Kelly, being teammates with a guy who thought he was larger than life because his father was a big-time lawyer and alumni, plus no more nine months of darkness.

"Don't get me wrong. I love D'Ville. But when it gets dark, people get real crazy. It's like living in another world. Like everyone is under some spell to do all types of wickedness, especially on Foolish Friday!"

Derrick remembered past Foolish Fridays watching the sunset, and people would just watch the stars light up the sky. Some may drink some Hyenna Lagers. Others will enjoy the nightlife or wait for daybreak. But everyone would be peaceful. Now I guess the more foolish you are, the more you fit in.

CHAPTER

5

The game was going as planned. D'Ville Street was winning by six points late in the first half. Derrick was playing the game of his life. He had twenty points and four assists—all to John, which surprised everyone, even John. Then Coach Kelly decided to sub in Spiff for Derrick.

It was one minute and thirty-five seconds left until halftime, so Derrick didn't mind. When Derrick approached the bench, he noticed Brad was looking in a daze. He looked like he had one too many Hyenna Lagers.

Brad's thoughts were all over the place. He wanted to play, but Coach Kelly noticed the strange look that had overtaken Brad's face. Coach also noticed how strange Brad was acting and thought to himself that he needed to sit out the first half. Brad started mumbling, "Movement tells all, but if you stand still, someone else could move you!" As soon as Brad finished his statement, the buzzer sounded, and it was halftime.

As both teams were walking toward their respected locker rooms, Derrick spotted Shavon. She imitated Derrick shooting a jump shot and then blew him a kiss. Derrick caught it and placed it on his chest. D'Ville St. maintained their six-point lead, but Battle Field College always played better in the second half.

When D'Ville St. had entered the locker room, Derrick was feeling like he was on cloud nine. Then out of the blue, John asked Derrick what he would do if he was unable to play basketball. Derrick became very tensed but tried to hide the feeling of not playing.

Basketball was the only thing that seemed to make sense to Derrick. Plus, he loved playing. John was tapping into Derrick's inner layer. He knew Derrick was a very passionate and driven individual. John was testing out chapter 6 of *The Strategy*. It was called "Deceptive Questioning."

Right after John asked Derrick that question, Coach Kelly informed the team who was starting the second half. Coach stated that Smoove, Spiff, John, Brad, and Smith were going in. Derrick had a puzzled look on his face, which quickly turned into anger.

Derrick exploded. He thought to himself, *How in the world could Coach bench his top scorer? I've even passed that wannabe Goldstein the ball, and he is benching me? OK, as soon as he put me in, I am going to go for mines, win the championship, then I am done with D'Ville St!*

CHAPTER

6

Coach Kelly knew deep down in his heart that what he was doing was wrong, but he also knew that life itself was a game coached by outside influences. Coach did not know if he could do this anymore. The job he once loved had all of a sudden become a burden. That was when he knew this was going to be the last time he would coach D'Ville St.

Just as the team was leaving the locker room, John's cell phone showed he had a text message. The message said, "Great shooting out there! But the game itself is played off the court! Continue to give Battlefield a blackout! "PS, don't worry about DA Other Man. Focus on the outcome!"

John gave that half smile like he already knew the outcome. *So far so good,* he thought to himself. *Twenty minutes away from a season of power, season of importance, season of mastering the strategy of movement, and becoming the most powerful force in the universe!*

Oh yeah, back to the game.

Battlefield College opened up with a six to zero run to start the second half. The arena could not understand why Coach Kelly benched Derrick to start the second half. Shavon looked at Derrick sitting on the bench with a towel over his head. She assumed that Derrick was crying, but when she saw his head rocking back and forth in rhythm, she knew it could only mean one thing. Derrick was about to show the world why he is DA Man.

Derrick was listening to his favorite song by BP3, "I'm a Monster, I'm a Gorilla, I'm a Beast." Derrick was waiting for Coach to call a timeout. Then he was going to put himself in and sub the weak link out.

Shavon also knew when DA Man enters Derrick, no one could control or reason with him. It's either his way or get out of the way. Shavon wasn't the only one watching Derrick. There was a full-figured woman who looked to overdressed to be at a basketball game. Shavon looked at the woman and expected her to some type of alumni. Then she realized that she was sitting in the cheap seats.

Finally, Coach Kelly called a timeout. And before the team came to the bench, Coach told Derrick that he was going back in the game. But what made Derrick smile was when Coach told him he was going in for John. D'Ville St. was losing by eight, but Smoove, Spiff, and Brad knew that DA Man has entered the building. Derrick gave John a pat on the back and whispered, "Watch DA Man lead us to the promised land." John just gave Derrick a half smile as Derrick and the other four players entered the game.

While the majority of D'Ville was at the arena, the rest of D'Ville was wandering around getting ready for Foolish Friday. Stan Goldstein was in his office watching the game and watching the sunset. "This is going to be a great Foolish Friday!" Goldstein stated. "So many people, so much stuff to get into. And when they get into trouble, they going to need representation."

Just as Goldstein was about to leave his office, he noticed someone was standing in front of his office with a huge briefcase. This woman was sitting in the lobby waiting for Stan to buzz her in. As Stan approached the lobby, he took out his cigar, lit it, and then let the mysterious woman in.

"Thanks for seeing me in such a short notice. I've heard that you was the best at what you do." Stan was looking at this woman the way a predator stalks its prey before they go in for the kill.

"Thank you, pretty lady! And winning cases is not the only thing I do best!" Stan replied.

"Well, Mr. Goldstein, as you can see, I'm all about the money! And what I have is high quality! So take this briefcase. Let's keep this conversation brief, and I let you know when or if I'm interested in your BOB boxers or briefs)!"

After Stan listened to this woman take control of the conversation, he was entangled in her web. "Ms. Bradshaw, I like your straightforward approach! You're a true business woman with sex appeal!" Stan said while blowing smoke rings in the air. Then Ms. Bradshaw dropped a card on Stan's desk and left out of his office walking in slow motion.

Stan watched Ms. Bradshaw walk and thought to himself how good it would feel to have his inner self dance with hers. As soon as Ms. Bradshaw left Good as Gold, she got in her car and drove to Trans Motor Boulevard.

Trans Motor Boulevard was forty miles north of Downtown D'Ville. Most of the so-called bottom feeders lived on this side of town. When D'Ville have their three months of daylight, it is OK. But it is a different story when Foolish Friday rolls around. The word in D'Ville is watch out when the sun goes down.

The locals say it is like walking in a whole new world. Plus, it's been said that the residents of the notorious Brady Tucker Projects lives by their own set of rules. If you are looking for some daylight saving time, a taste of the nightlife, daybreak, or some Dungeon Dragons, then go over down to Trans Motor Boulevard. But the boulevard is possessed with the Brady Tuckers who love to cause a Rucker.

Back at the arena, D'Ville St. was two minutes and sixteen seconds left from winning the championship. Derrick, a.k.a. Da Man, had the crowd chanting, "DA, DA, DA is Da Man!" The energy flowing through the arena was incredible. John was feeding off the energy and looked at this mysterious man who was sitting with all the elite figures of D'Ville.

John also noticed how the man gave a certain hand signal, and all of a sudden, certain people in the crowd began to do the wave. Then out of nowhere, Coach Kelly told John to go into the game for Derrick.

As Derrick saw John approaching the scorer's table, he noticed someone or something standing next to him. The figure seemed to be dark like a shadow. Now Derrick knew his mind wasn't playing tricks on him, but his lost of focus caused D'Ville St. the ball. Derrick had passed the ball out of bounds, now John had entered the game.

Derrick was in shock when he found out John was coming in the game for him. It was forty seconds left, and D'Ville St. was down by one. Coach knew Derrick was exhausted for getting D'Ville St. back in the game. Plus, Coach noticed Derrick was not playing team ball.

His alter ego as Da Man was starting to hurt the team more than help it. *As you can see, Coach Kelly is trying his best from keeping me grounded!* Derrick thought to himself. *At this point, I don't care if D'Ville St. win or lose at this point. I've played my last game at D'Ville St."*

Plus, Derrick figured he got the attention of the GBA to become a top-ten draft pick. But Derrick didn't realize that he got another individual's attention with his superior play. As the clock was winding down to zero, Derrick noticed someone watching him from the crowd.

At first, he thought the man in the business suit was a scout, but when he noticed the ring on his right ring finger, he knew it could only be one person. It was no other than Percy Sanders, better known in D'Ville as PS. Derrick began to put the pieces together to make sense of the whole situation.

"Coach Kelly's last-second lineup changed, being substituted out with forty seconds left in the game, Brad acting out of character, and John giving me that half smile when I went back in the game! Derrick thought to himself.

While enjoying the game, a sudden jingle came from his inside pocket. PS checked his phone and noticed that his delivery had been made. Then PS began to focus on his next move, as Foolish Friday was approaching.

PS was trying to put together a group of investors to bring a professional basketball team to D'Ville. The D'Ville Deceptions was going to be the name, and Derrick was the player, Mr. Sanders had his eye on to lead them to his promised land.

Now it was ten seconds left in the game, and D'Ville St. was down by one. Derrick still couldn't believe he was on the bench. Battlefield College was playing a three-two zone, which prevented Smoove to pass the ball to John. So Smoove went to his second option, which was Brad under the basket. Smoove passed it to him.

Brad caught the ball, but when he went up to dunk it, he saw this dark shadow figure sitting on top of the basket. Brad just stopped dead in his tracks and did the most bizarre thing. Brad decided to throw the basketball at the so-called shadowlike figure. But everyone in D'Ville Arena looked stunned as Brad threw the game away.

I know I didn't see what I just saw! What in the world was Brad thinking? I hope he got paid more than enough to pull that stunt! Does he even know the kind of heat is going to get in D'Ville? Derrick thought to himself. Then everyone went from being angry to becoming excited about tonight's sunset at D'Ville Square.

CHAPTER

7

"The time is almost near, my fellow shadows!" MD 20/20 has stated. "This is the time we gain another month of darkness!" MD 20/20 told all his shadows that he wanted them to cause as much deception, destruction, and, if they get the chance, even death. He also warned them to beware of J. Boogie and his GL's.

MD 20/20 knew that J. Boogie was well aware of their evil plan, and they were ready to reclaim their territory by any means necessary. After MD 20/20 gave his instructions, all three thousand shadows where itching to go up to the surface and make their master proud.

Back in the D'Ville St. locker room, the whole team just watched Brad have a nervous breakdown. Brad kept saying, "Beware of the night. Beware of the night. The big bad Shadow took away my flight!" The team doctors took Brad to D'Ville Hospital for observations and safety precautions from the citizens of D'Ville.

Too many strange events were taking place in these past two hours. Derrick looked at Spiff and thought about their conversation before the game. Derrick was beginning to seriously believe there was someone or something bigger than this so-called system of life.

Spiff began to cry as he saw Brad being taken to the hospital. Spiff called the team together to say a private request of protection to the

24

Master of The Universe. Even John was a little shaken up with Brad's strange behavior. He had no idea that Brad would react in that manner.

John was also curious how deep Brad was into reading *The Strategy*. He asked himself, "*Did he follow the guidelines? Did he skip chapters in order to gain power? Or was he trying to tap into my plan?* John knew he had to visit Brad and find out the cause of his mental deceleration.

After the game, Shavon decided to surprise Derrick with a romantic dinner for two at her place. She left Derrick a text message when the game was over.

"After watching Brad lost control like that, I felt that I had to be around so sanity. I know Spiff wanted me to go with him to this day walker thing, but I just want to be to myself right now! I wonder what the apple of my eye is doing," Derrick said to himself.

Just when Derrick was about to call Shavon, he noticed she left him a text message. *That's what I'm talking about, baby!* Derrick thought to himself. He needed his Von-Von tonight, and now he had a reason not to go with Spiff.

Smoove walked over to Spiff and asked him if he was OK. Spiff gave Smoove a half smile as he wiped a tear from the corner of his eye. "Yeah, I'm fine. Just got a little emotional about the game!" Spiff replied. Smoove knew something wasn't right about today's outcome—how the game ended, what happened to Brad, and the way Derrick was acting.

Smoove knew that Spiff was a dedicated day walker and was hoping he could shine some light on this situation. John, all of a sudden, felt Smoove's mixture of fear and hidden insecurity.

So John decided to send a hidden message to Spiff that would make Spiff defensive to any of Smoove's questions. When John saw Spiff all of a sudden start rushing out of the locker room to avoid Smoove, he knew he was definitely on to something. Thanks to *The Strategy*.

As the sun was getting closer and closer to going into hibernation, Spiff was sitting in his room having his usual private conversation with the Master of The Universe. Spiff was concerned for his friends. Spiff thought about the strange events that were already taking place. He could sense the aura of ignorance, making its presence known.

Spiff turned to page 91 from *The Good Book* to get him elevated. Now Spiff was ready to go to the day walker revival and listen to Finder O'Johnson at the foundation.

In the skies above, J. Boogie was watching how MD 20/20 himself was able to reach the surface before dark. When MD 20/20 himself sat on the rim in the final seconds of the championship game, J. Boogie knew someone has tapped into his strategic art of deception. J. Boogie knew that it didn't come from Mr. Sanders.

It came from a new player in this game called DOEOL (Day or Dark Element of Life). J. Boogie had to change his entire game plan— thanks to this new player's sudden movements.

Shavon and Derrick were enjoying each other's rhythm of love as the smooth sounds of Larry Black were circulating through the air. Shavon knew that Derrick needed his Von-Von to get him through this tough and exhausting day.

She also sensed that there was something about Derrick. Normally he pours out his heart, and Shavon's ears are the cups that receive his words. But Derrick decided to keep quiet and just let his mind replay the last couple of weeks of strange events.

From the unexpected invite to John's house that kept him from walking into a bank robbery, Spiff's phone call before the game—that personal voice that told him to leave the hotel room—it was too much for Derrick to digest and make sense of.

Shavon's phone rang, which snapped Derrick out of his trance. Derrick noticed Shavon trying to talk real low, thinking Derrick was sleeping. As soon as Shavon hung up, Derrick got up and told Shavon he felt he needed some time to himself. She couldn't believe what Derrick had just said to her. Shavon's plan was to watch the sunset together, and then she was going to surprise Derrick with two tickets to Paradise Island for spring break. She wanted to get away from the darkness of D'Ville, even if it was only for one week.

After meeting with her employees at Trans Motor Boulevard, Ms. Bradshaw went to Club Blackout to make sure everything was ready for tonight's festivities. Ms. Bradshaw told the staff that Mr. Sanders was expecting nothing less than perfection tonight. "This is the biggest night of the year, and Mr. Sanders hates to be made a fool out of!" stated Ms. Bradshaw.

Right on cue, PS walked in with Mr. Goldstein and the hottest hip-hop artist BP3. BP3 agreed to perform live as well as Civilian SlegeHammer. As the clock strikes twelve, there should be a packed house spending all their money enjoying the foolishness of darkness.

CHAPTER

8

Spiff decided to visit Brad before he went to the day walker revival. Something on the inside would not let Spiff begin to walk in the hospital. Spiff noticed D'Ville Police had the entrance blocked off out of fear of someone trying to harm Brad. Spiff took it as a sign from the Master of The Universe that his friend is in good hands and could continue on his journey of elevation.

As Finder O'Johnson was getting ready for the day walker revival, he received a surprise visit from Shavon. "Hey, Finder. I got here as fast as I could, but I couldn't get Derrick to come with me," Shavon stated as she was trying to catch her breath. Shavon saw the dark shadow that caught Brad's attention. She was hoping Derrick would be able to explain what happened, but it seemed that something or someone had total control of their movements.

Shavon could not make any sense of their sexual episode that took place not too long ago. Finder O'Johnson advised Shavon to stay for the revival, but she declined, making up an excuse that she was tired, and she needed to rest.

Back at Club Blackout, PS was discussing his plans with Mr. Goldstein. The plan was to bring a professional basketball team to D'Ville. PS already had an eye on who he could build his dynasty around. Stan assumed that PS was talking about his son. PS just smiled because he already knew that his lawyer thought he was referring to his son.

Yeah, PS promised 5 percent ownership and legal representation of the franchise, but that was just to secure the approval of the GBA officials to grant him the team. Sanders's real plan was to have the team be sponsored by Fizz Energy Drink and buyout Good as Goldstein Law Firm. Sanders, already an interesting man of wealth, was more focused at being in total control and become the ultimate strategist.

When PS finished signing the documents, Monique walked into the club. She walked over to PS and laid the briefcase down on the table. Stan pulled out a $100 bill, crumpled it up, and threw it down on the floor. Mr. Sanders noticed what Stan was just up to, so he gave Monique the signal to get the money. As Monique walked over to the crumpled $100 bill, she made sure that Stan got what he thought was his money's worth by watching Monique get the money.

Man, what in the world is going on? What is Shavon up to? And why did she leave the bedroom to talk to whoever that was on her phone? I already lost the most important game in my life, witnessed my friend and teammate lose his mind, and she pulls this stunt! It's cool. I'm just going to smoke a Dungeon Dragon or two, sip on some Hyenna Lagers, might even enjoy the nightlife and just black out!

Stop thinking about Foolish Friday, Spiff, Shavon, day walkers, night crawlers, bottom feeders—whatever! I'm Derrick DA Man Arthur, and I think the world needs to know who is the star of the show!

And once the sunset, I'm about to focus on what's best for me! No more D'Ville St., Coach Kelly, and definitely you don't have to worry about that punk John Goldstein!

Spiff noticed Shavon running out of Finder O'Johnson's office. Spiff yelled out to her, but Shavon just kept running like Spiff didn't even exist. Spiff just shrugged and thought nothing of it. He was focused on getting prepared for the nine months of darkness.

All of a sudden, the foundation of voices made their entrance into the lighthouse. Then they began to get the crowd into it with their beautiful singing. As Finder O'Johnson came in, everyone started clapping, stomping, and screaming, "Give us the day and destroy the night! I choose to walk and not lose my sight!"

Then Finder O'Johnson told the audience that they can take a seat. Spiff could not wait to hear the word of protection. Spiff began to visualize himself being a finder and continue to fight the good fight of overcoming the people of the night.

D'Ville Square was packed. So many people from all over D'Ville came to watch the sunset. Some of the women in the crowd started flashing the D'Ville Police. The men was hooting, hollering, and whistling, as they were trying to get a sneak peek. But the D'Ville Police arrested the women and told them they might get sent to B-Have County.

Then one of the police officers said, "For the right price and if they obey? We could look the other way at this offense!" The women knew they couldn't afford the bail, so they did whatever the officers requested.

Look at those exterminators! Already getting their taste of the night, and it is not even eleven thirty. Man, these so-called officers is a joke! Oh well, it is not my problem. Nobody told those bottom feeders to show off their vitamin D's to the whole world! Derrick said in his thoughts as he inhaled the smoke from his Dungeon Dragon.

Then Derrick felt a vibrating sensation in his pocket. He was so caught in his thoughts he didn't realize that Smoove was calling him. "Hello, Earth to Derrick, or should I say DA Man!" Finally, Derrick snapped out of his trance and laughed at Smoove's comment. Smoove had some Hyenna Lagers and was looking for Derrick so they could go to Club Blackout.

Derrick and Smoove couldn't stop laughing as they watched people trying to sneak in the club with no avail. There was this one guy who thought he could just walk past security like he owned the club. When the six-foot-four, three-hundred-pound muscular security guard attempted to grab the guy, this man instantly began to break-dance but ended up breaking his leg. He tried to get up just to have his body come crashing down hard to the pavement.

Finally, D'Ville Police came and arrested the man for whatever reason they felt was suitable. "The poor guy was feeling the nightlife and didn't know how to behave!" stated Sergeant Lang. Sergeant Lang looked forward to Foolish Fridays, especially when he can use his ways on making the citizens of D'Ville behave.

"Sergeant Lang was responsible for sending at least seventy-five people to Behave County last Foolish Friday!" whispered a woman waiting in line. Then Derrick thought about his encounter with Sergeant Lang when he was a freshman. Derrick was walking on Trans Motor Boulevard when he noticed a car following him. Sergeant Lang was just a patrolman then, but he was always looking for someone to help him get up the chain of command. So he would patrol up and down Trans Motor Boulevard to use the bottom feeders by sending them to Behave County and himself to the top of the D'Ville extermination.

Back at the day walker revival, Finder O'Johnson had all the day walkers fired up with the word of protection. Finder O'Johnson stated to the crowd, "The time is now to put an end to all of this foolishness!" Finder O'Johnson claimed that as day walkers, they are responsible to shine light all through the night.

The crowd became more and more charged up after every word Finder O'Johnson said. Spiff was just looking at everyone and began to say to himself, "These people don't even realize how fierce this task is! O'Johnson needs to stop pumping these people up and prepare them for these next nine months of craziness!"

As Spiff was visualizing himself being the finder, he was broken from his trance when he noticed who walked in the lighthouse. It was Andy Schwartz, but everybody in D'Ville knew him as Ruthless. He was the leader of the Explorers, a very organized and most feared group of individuals who gets their point across very physically. The last time Ruthless was seen in D'Ville, he had gotten into a scuffle with some of the Brady Tucker fellas, and unfortunately, one of them lost his life.

"What is that Barberian doing in here?" stated Ms. Barber.

"The light will never shine on that monster," whispered the elder man sitting three seats from Spiff.

When Finder O'Johnson noticed what all the hoopla was about, he asked everyone in the lighthouse to hold hands and thank the Master of The Universe for shining his light and giving them night vision. Spiff couldn't stop looking at Andy. He knew that this Foolish Friday was going to be different, but nobody saw this one coming.

After everyone gave thanks for receiving night vision, Andy asked Finder O'Johnson if he could he remove his shades. Every person in the lighthouse got real silent, waiting to see what Finder O'Johnson was going to say. Finder O'Johnson had doubts about letting Ruthless reveal his story and began a new day. Then the Master of The Universe spoke to Finder O'Johnson through J. Boogie, telling him to "let go and let that man come clean!"

When the lighthouse saw that Finder O'Johnson approved of Andy removing his shades, half of the lighthouse made threats that they will not walk in the light with an explorer. An *explorer* is a term the members of the lighthouse use when they feel a person isn't committed to being a day walker.

Back on campus, all the students at D'Ville St. were walking around, enjoying the nightlife as they were looking to see what kind of mischief they could get into. It's like when the sun goes down, this newfound energy overwhelms everyone, and people just lose control of themselves. Last year, one student thought it was a good idea to mix Hyenna Lager with Fizz Energy Drinks, pop some D pills, and smoke some Dungeon Dragons one hour before the sunset. The student claimed he wanted to experience daybreak but never woke up. He passed out in his room after partying all night from dehydration.

After that incident, D'Ville Police sent any and every minor that possessed D pills, Dungeon Dragons, or any other nonstore substance away to D'Ville Detention Center. Then Sergeant Lang would send the minors to the Ultra Dome after they left the D'Ville Detention Center. The Ultra Dome was ten times worse than being sent to B-Have County. Rumor has it that Sergeant Lang was giving at least ten to twenty-five years to people like it was candy.

Shavon was walking through campus with her head down and feeling defeated. She kept questioning why Derrick would just get up and leave her apartment like that. Just as she was about to go inside, she heard a strange but soothing voice call out to her. When she turned around and saw who called out to her, she wanted to run inside her apartment. Then it seemed like she was under the control of this strange and soothing voice. Shavon just stood there motionless. She felt this new sensation flow through her body as the strange voice came closer. Shavon was hoping that this was Derrick acting like their favorite singer Larry Black, but when she turned around, she couldn't believe who was standing there, making her feel like more than a woman.

Back at Club Blackout, Derrick and Smoove were enjoying the so-called star treatment they were receiving. All the females from D'Ville were plotting on how they were going to leave with the new so-called superstars. Derrick's mind was all over the place. He still couldn't understand why Shavon went into the other room to speak on the phone, what was going on with Brad, and what Spiff said to him before the game. Today's events couldn't escape his thoughts no matter how much he tried to drink it away.

Derrick was drinking glasses of Redemption like there was no tomorrow. Smoove decided to roll another Dungeon Dragon and enjoy the energy of the night. Just as Smoove was about to put fire to his Dungeon Dragon, he noticed a beautiful woman approaching him and Derrick. The woman was holding an envelope that was addressed to Derrick and Smoove. Derrick didn't know what to make of it, but when he felt the weight of the envelope, he knew that it could only contain one thing.

As the nurse walked out of room 212, she noticed something strange walking through the hallway. She began to page the front desk when all of a sudden, she found herself trapped in the staircase. She couldn't reenter into the second floor because she didn't have her card key. Then all of a sudden, the lights in the staircase went out, and this dark and terrifying voice said, "Nurse Rebecca, the doctor is waiting to make his rounds!" Nurse Rebecca tried to use her G-phone as a light but couldn't see the person speaking to her. Then she felt the coldest set of hands touch every inch of her body, which made the hairs on the back of her neck stand straight up.

The voice whispered in Nurse Rebecca's ear, "What's wrong, sweetheart? You don't like it when Daddy touches you like that? Just pretend that I'm Dr. Richardson!" Nurse Rebecca started beating on the door and screaming for someone to help. The dark voice looked into Nurse Rebecca's eyes to show her having sexual relations with Dr. Richardson and other married men. Then she saw those same eyes turn red, and then she realized who this dark voice was.

Rebecca thought back to the stories her grandmother would tell her about the body snatcher. She told Rebecca to be careful about crawling from one body to the next, or she could become the next one snatched up. Then Rebecca closed her eyes and tried to have a conversation with the Master of The Universe.

"He can't save you from this, Nurse. He is operating on another patient right now! Plus, you don't have day walker insurance!" stated the dark voice. Nurse Rebecca felt her clothes being ripped off, and then she felt herself being separated from her ultimate being with every forceful stroke from MD 20/20. When MD 20/20 was finished, he picked up Nurse Rebecca's G-phone and disguised his voice to sound like her. MD 20/20 had the front desk buzz him and Shadow No. 26 on to the second floor of the hospital.

"Now it's time to cause some death, destruction, and deception, right, all wicked one?" asked Shadow No. 26.

"Be patient, my slave! You got so much to learn. You stupid shadow!" said MD 20/20.

When MD 20/20 and Shadow No. 26 approached room 212, MD 20/20 paused and smelled the doorknob. MD 20/20 could smell Brad's fear and was ready to have a conversation with him. Then all of a sudden, a blue force field covered the door. MD 20/20 told Shadow No.

26 to go in first. When Shadow No. 26 touched the door, his hands began to melt. MD 20/20 began to laugh hysterically.

He knew the blue force field came from the Master of The Universe and wanted to show how stupid Shadow No. 26 was. Then MD 20/20 and Shadow No. 26 returned to the world below.

When Derrick and Smoove opened their envelope, they couldn't believe how much money they got. Both of them got at least $50,000 each and a personal note attached. The note said, "There are times in life when the lessons you learn will not be in a classroom! And what you think is real is only a deception! PS."

Derrick read the card at least three times. He knew it was some type of riddle, but what did it mean? Then all of a sudden, Ms. Bradshaw approached Derrick and Smoove. She explained how Mr. Sanders wanted to meet with them, and he wasn't taking no for an answer.

As the clock showed that it was one in the morning, Sergeant Lang and the D'Ville Police thought it was time to do their street rips. Sergeant Lang took his special E-Force Team with him to Trans Motor Boulevard, with it being Foolish Friday. He knew he could get as many bottom feeders to B-Have County, or they will get the ultimate punishment.

Trans Motor Boulevard was filled with people. If you were looking for a good time, a taste of the nightlife, waiting for daylight saving time, this was the place to be. Tricky and Showdown were making sure all the bottom feeders were staying grounded. The exterminators from D'Ville Police Department got what they came to claim and made sure the night crawlers kept crawling.

Tricky and Showdown had to keep a lookout for those exterminators from D'Ville Police Department and the Examples. As hard as D'Ville Police Department wanted to nail them, they always seemed to be two steps ahead of them. Now the examples just wanted to take away Trans Motor Boulevard for their own reasons of interest. The Explorers saw how profitable D'Ville could be if they had complete control of the boulevard. The Explorers had a vision of making D'Ville the highest-grossing place during the times of darkness by taking advantage of the people at night.

Back at the day walker revival, Spiff had a strange feeling that something or someone was after Brad. He felt a strong urge to have a private conversation with J. Boogie while Andy was removing his shades. Spiff knew that he had to get to Brad and shine some light on him. Finder O'Johnson was putting the finishing touches on his words of wisdom. He explained that the only way they were going to receive more light was to expose the works of the dark head-on. How? They must stay focused, and the Master of The Universe would prevail. Every day walker in the lighthouse began to shout, scream, and jump up and down, ready to prove that they can overcome the night. Spiff and Andy both knew that it was going to take more than a three-hour revival to overcome the works of MD 20/20 and the world below.

Back on campus, Amy noticed Shavon engaged in a conversation with John Goldstein. Now Amy couldn't believe that she would ever cheat on Derrick. "If all the people in the world, to cheat on Derrick with! Why would she choose his worst enemy?" Amy said to herself as she continued to watch them from Shavon's window. All of a sudden, Amy began to feel this warm sensation flow through her body.

As she made eye contact with John, she had this strong desire to want to become one with him. The more she looked at him, the more intense this feeling took over Amy. Next thing you know, Amy began to explore herself as she visualized John making her feel like more than a woman.

Amy was broken out of her trance when she heard Shavon come in. Amy couldn't believe that she was half naked sitting by the window, feeling like she just made love to her exact opposite.

John left campus knowing he was getting stronger with the help of *The Strategy.* He laughed at how he was able to have an outer-body experience while having a conversation with Shavon at the same time. *It's just a matter of time before I'm the most feared man in D'Ville! People everywhere, beware!* John thought to himself on his way to Club Blackout.

When Spiff left the day walker revival, he was more in a state of confusion than peace. *Something didn't feel right tonight!* Spiff thought to himself. Spiff felt that Finder O'Johnson was leading the day walkers on a suicide mission, and he didn't know what to make of Ruthless removing his shades. Spiff knew that in the back of his mind, Ruthless is not to be trusted. Only time would tell what lies ahead now that the moon has risen.

Back at D'Ville Hospital, Brad had a flashlight pointed directly at the door in his room. Brad just knew that someone or something was in his room. He wanted to make sure he would see everyone who tries to enter his room. Brad wasn't taking any chances of sitting by himself in the dark. The doctors felt Brad needed to get some sleep, so they cut off all the lights on the second floor. And the batteries in Brad's flashlight went dead. So Brad was alone in the dark.

Nurse Rebecca had felt sorry for Brad and gave him the flashlight. She also noticed how he was looking right past her as if he could see someone or something else was in the room with them. She thought nothing of it and couldn't wait to have dinner and a little dessert with Dr. Richardson. When Nurse Rebecca exited Brad's room, Brad heard a collection of voices, saying, "If only she knew what awaits her on the other side!"

As Ms. Bradshaw poured a glass of Redemption for Derrick and Smoove, Derrick began to replay all the weird events that just transpired. First, he and Smoove got paid at least $50,000, Brad losing his mind, Shavon starting to have secret conversations with someone else after she became one with Derrick. Finally, Derrick was broken out of his train thought when his phone started ringing. Derrick sent the call straight to voicemail and just wanted to enjoy the night.

Ten minutes later, PS entered the room in his all-black suit with the gold tie to match his custom-made gold and black frames. Mr. Sanders had the letters *BV* engraved on the side of both lens. Derrick felt a little uneasy about this situation. Smoove, on the other hand, was cool and calm as usual. Letting the effects of the Dungeon Dragons, Hyenna Lagers, and the glasses of Redemption take effect.

PS felt that Derrick was in a confused state of mind and knew he would be the perfect man for his master plan. PS also noticed how calm Smoove was. He never felt anything like it.

Ms. Bradshaw noticed Smoove checking out her lovely assets and decided to put on a little show for him. Smoove was definitely enjoying the view, until Derrick nudged him and told him to stay focused.

"Something got your attention, Mr. Rodgers?" asked PS, as he noticed Smoove watching Ms. Bradshaw from a distance. Derrick gave Smoove a mean stare to let him know that Mr. Sanders was very observant of everything going on around him. Ms. Bradshaw just winked as she walked off into the night.

Just as Mr. Sanders was about to explain why he called Derrick and Smoove to his private booth, Derrick noticed John and Stan Goldstein entered the club. Derrick's heart began to beat real fast as he followed John's every move. PS saw the intense look Derrick showed and began to calm him down without saying a word. PS knew there was something about Derrick, and it was a lot deeper than his skills on the basketball court.

The energy that was flowing throughout the private booth was incredible. PS just rubbed his hands together and thought to himself, *By this time next year, I will be the ultimate strategist! And everyone from D'Ville to Paradise City will bow down to me!*

Once Stan Goldstein barged his way into PS's private booth, the mood turned sour. Stan was being his typical obnoxious self, talking about how he could have any bottom feeder and have his way with them for the right price. PS put one finger in the air to silence Stan and dismissed Derrick, Smoove, and John from the booth. John just looked back at his father and put his head down in shame, as he just exposed who was in charge.

As Derrick and Smoove were leaving the booth, they both noticed a group of night crawlers doing explicit acts with some of the members of the D'Ville Police. Sergeant Lang was sniffing some night life off the back side of the almond-complexioned night crawler. Smoove took out his G-Phone and decided to record the entertaining encounter. Derrick felt he had enough excitement for one Foolish Friday. He told Smoove that he was heading back to campus, but Smoove had other plans. Smoove wanted to end the night becoming one with the money.

When Derrick got back on campus, he immediately called Shavon. Derrick was feeling real good about himself after a couple of glasses of Redemption, not to mention the Dungeon Dragons he smoked and Hyenna Lagers he drank. He was hoping he could release his self before the yellow moon rises. Once Derrick noticed that Shavon wasn't answering, he hung up his phone and decided to put an end to his Foolish Friday as he went to sleep.

CHAPTER

10

Shavon was in the shower trying to wash the night away. She didn't like how John was able to touch her inner being by just having a casual conversation. But she really couldn't understand how Derrick could just leave without saying a word and then send his phone straight to voicemail when she tried to call him. Shavon thought to herself, *Now I would be wrong if I just blew him off, like he didn't mean anything to me! Now he thinks he could call me after 3:00 a.m., and I'm supposed to answer? DA Man is about to find out that he is dealing with a true woman of elevation!* Just before Shavon went to sleep, she sent Derrick a text that read, "Let the games begin!"

Dr. Richardson had received another phone call at 3:00 a.m. Mrs. Richardson decided to see who was calling her husband this late. When she saw the pictures of her husband becoming one with Nurse Rebecca, it made her sick to her stomach.

Then this smooth-talking voice began to whisper in Mrs. Richardson's ear, "Hey, Sophie. Who does this guy think he is? After all the sacrifices you made so he could advance his career! You had a chance to be a senior partner at Handover, Handover, and Handover, but you had Robert Jr. and became a full-time housewife! Now Dr. Richardson thinks he can play doctor with every and anybody and have you looked like a fool like your first husband Peter. You remember Peter, the one who left you to raise your daughter all by yourself? Now I know you not going to let another man make you look silly, right, Sophie?"

By the time Mrs. Richardson finished listening to MD2 0/20 stir her emotions, Mrs. Richardson went into the kitchen, grabbed a knife, and began to carve into Dr. Richardson's chest. "Fool me once, shame on you. Fool me twice, shame on me!" Dr. Richardson tried to fight his wife off, as she repeatedly carved the words into his chest. He noticed he was being held down by a group of shadows, and his wife possessed the most evil-looking, bloodshot red eyes any man had ever seen.

When Dr. Richardson was removed from his ultimate being, MD 20/20 showed him how much fun it was to trick his wife into killing him and how he could torture him and Nurse Rebecca for their act in house division. Dr. Richardson still watched his wife continue to carve into a motionless body. Robert Jr. is going to wonder why Mom killed Dad, and Alicia is already addicted to the nightlife. Another household ruined—thanks to the works of foolishness.

Derrick woke up and read what Shavon had text him. Derrick felt a sudden urge to text her back, saying they were over but decided to text back: "Let DA best man win!"

In D'Ville Hospital, the after-hours supervisor noticed that Dr. Richardson didn't show up for his 3:00 a.m. shift. Then he paged Nurse Rebecca to prep a patient for an emergency at 6:00 a.m. When the night supervisor didn't get a response, he thought to himself, *I have to do something about the unprofessionalism between Dr. Richardson and Nurse Rebecca. Maybe I'll report them to the board of hospital directors and get that pretty boy terminated once and for all! He thinks he is God's gift to women!*

Then the night supervisor checked the patient log and saw that Nurse Rebecca was assigned to check out the spooked-out patients on the second floor. He turned on the security monitors on all the second-floor rooms, staff bathrooms, and hidden staircases, hoping to catch Nurse Rebecca and Dr. Richardson red-handed. But what he found was more than he had asked for.

The night supervisor called D'Ville Police to report that one of his staff members was literally ripped in half at the midsection and lower back region.

Coach Kelly couldn't make any sense of what happened in the game last night. "What was going on with Brad? Why didn't I listen to my inner being?" Coach Kelly poured another glass of Redemption and looked at the picture of his ex-wife Gloria and son Christopher. Coach Kelly was a devoted day walker until four years ago when he lost his son.

Christopher loved the game of basketball just like his dad, but he also loved the nightlife. Christopher would have been twenty-three years old this past Friday. Coach Kelly and Christopher had a huge fight on his birthday four years ago. Coach Kelly wanted Christopher to go with him to the day walker revival, but Gloria called Coach Kelly a stick in the mud. Then she took Christopher down to D'Ville Square to watch the sunset. While the sun was making its exit, Gloria gave Christopher the white powder and a straw and wished him a happy birthday. Christopher got his first taste of the nightlife. And three years later, it would be his last.

The night supervisor was being interrogated by Sergeant Lang. Sergeant Lang could smell the fear coming from the night supervisor. As Sergeant Lang kept looking at the video footage, he noticed that Nurse Rebecca was attacked by a second party. Sergeant Lang began to suspect that the night supervisor had something to do with it, but he saw that the second party involved looked almost not human. Sergeant Lang just came from Dr. Richardson's house after he got the word that his wife just snapped and killed her husband. Sergeant Lang knew someone or something was behind this. And when he cracked the case, he knew he was going straight to the top of the D'Ville Police chain.

CHAPTER

11

In the skies above, the Master of The Universe watched how MD 20/20 made his first move. "So eager but yet so desperate to win!" the Master of The Universe said to himself. J. Boogie just sat there, waiting patiently for his instructions. J. Boogie couldn't understand why the master would let Nurse Rebecca and Dr. Richardson die without giving them a warning, but he also wouldn't dare question his father's decision either. J. Boogie felt sorry for Nurse Rebecca becoming a night crawler. It happened when she was fifteen years old. She thought it was cool to go to a college party that her nineteen-year-old boyfriend was throwing at that time. Rebecca had too many Hyenna Lagers to drink, and her boyfriend, plus five others, took advantage of the situation.

Since then, Rebecca dealt with men on her terms. No relationships, just one-on-one encounters. J. Boogie tried to answer her grandmother's private conversations, but it seemed like the influences of confusion had too much of a stronghold on her.

MD 20/20 knew how to kill two birds with one stone by using Dr. Richardson who made one too many house calls to numerous women who all happened to be married. Who would have thought that Dr. Richardson would be killed by his own wife.

When J. Boogie received his instructions on how to counterattack MD 20/20 and his shadows, then he sent a feather down and placed it on Derrick's pillow and gathered up as many as one hundred GL's to go down to midlevel.

Man, what was I thinking! I've got to be crazy to let my pride get in the way. Sometimes I wonder about myself! Derrick thought as he kept staring at Shavon's text message. He felt very vulnerable every time he read the words: "Let the games begin!" All Derrick could think about was how much she knew all his movements. "I guess I got to become the game changer to prove that I'm the man in this relationship!" Derrick said to himself.

Just as Derrick was about to leave his room, he noticed a strange-looking feather on his pillow. Derrick took a picture of it and sent it to Smoove. He wrote very funny message to Mr. Rodgers: "That was messed up to make me believe I slept with a pigeon."

Spiff had a hard time trying to come to grips that Ruthless wanted to become a day walker. Spiff knew that deep down, he should be happy that the Master of The Universe led him to remove his shades. Plus, he couldn't stop thinking about Brad. Spiff picked up his G-Phone and called the hospital. He just wanted to make sure his friend was all right after that meltdown he suffered in the locker room. Spiff's ultimate being wasn't at peace, so he decided to have a conversation with J. Boogie.

Back at Club Blackout, Smoove was putting on his clothes. He watched Ms. Bradshaw put on her black silk robe and handed him the envelope. Smoove counted the money and realized that he was missing $10,000. Smoove had a puzzled look on his face, and then Ms. Bradshaw said, "Baby, this ride costs! Nothing personal. just business!"

Then Smoove's response was "I would kiss you goodbye, but I can't afford it!" Ms. Bradshaw walked over to Smoove kiss him on the lips and said, "But I also take credit!" Smoove was let out the back door and continued on his journey back to campus.

John woke up this morning feeling like a new man. After putting his plan into play, he knew that with the right woman by his side, nothing could stop him. John had only one woman in mind, and that was Shavon. John always had a secret crush on her but never had the courage to approach her until last night.

Coach Kelly couldn't stop thinking about his son. Something on the inside was telling Coach that he needed to have a conversation with the Master of The Universe. Just as he was about to close his eyes, the phone rang.

It just happened to be Sergeant Lang giving Coach an update on what happened at the hospital. Sergeant Lang informed him that Brad could be a suspect of the murder of Nurse Rebecca. Brad was the last person she talked to before she was murdered. Since D'Ville Police wasn't able to reach his parents, they asked Coach Kelly to come and pick him up until they are ready to question him. Coach Kelly agreed to pick him up.

What's all the commotion going on out here? How come Dr. Richardson or Nurse Rebecca haven't come by this morning? Brad couldn't contain the thoughts racing through his mind at what seemed to feel like it was going one hundred miles per hour. Brad couldn't eat or sleep ever since he was admitted into the hospital. All he kept seeing was that scary-looking dark creature with those soul-emptying eyes. He knew he couldn't fall asleep out of fear that he would see those horrifying red eyes. Then all of a sudden, Brad's hospital door opened. Brad decided to pretend that he was asleep. His plan was to surprise who ever approached him and hit them with the flashlight Nurse Rebecca gave him; but when he overheard Coach Kelly talking to Sergeant Lang, he decided not to follow through with his plan.

Derrick met up with Smoove and Spiff at D'Ville Diner. Smoove and Spiff were sitting at their usual booth in the back. Derrick always felt good when he had his usual sausage and cheddar cheese omelet with strawberry pancakes. Smoove couldn't stop smiling. Spiff asked, "What are you so happy about?"

Smoove pulled out a pair of TSV designer shades and said, "It feels good to lay in a pile of money!" Spiff just shook his head in disgust. He thought Smoove was talking about taking money, but Derrick exactly what and who Smoove was talking about. Smoove was referring to his private encounter with Ms. Bradshaw, a.k.a. the Money.

Just when Derrick was taking his second bite from his strawberry pancakes, Spiff asked them if they did have a personal conversation with J. Boogie. Smoove acted like he didn't hear Spiff, but Derrick couldn't even look at Spiff's direction. Spiff sensed the unexpected tension and decided to change the subject. Then out of nowhere, Shavon entered the diner with her cousin Amy. Smoove waved Shavon and Amy to sit with them. Shavon, to their surprise, looked Derrick dead in the eyes and shook her head no. Smoove was dumbfounded with Shavon's reaction. But what really surprised him was how calm, cool, and collective Derrick was about the whole situation.

When Derrick finished eating, he got up from the both, put a $100 bill on the table, and said, "Breakfast is on *me*!" He looked straight into Smoove's eyes. Then Derrick made his exit out of the diner without even looking in Shavon's direction. Shavon was hurt but refused to show it because she knew that in order to win the game, you must have a good strategy.

After becoming a day walker, Ruthless decided to take a stroll down Trans Motor Boulevard. Little did he know that someone was watching his every move. Ms. Bradshaw couldn't believe her eyes. She just knew Ruthless was supposed to be sentenced to B-Have County for another twenty sunsets. She thought about getting his attention by beeping her car horn, but she told herself to "stay focus. You got important business to handle." Ruthless felt that someone was watching him. Then from a distance, he heard a familiar voice call out to him.

"There is only one cat daddy who is bold enough to walk down this street before they explore it!" Ruthless turned around and was greeted by his longtime friend Tricky.

"Hey, man. What it look like?" said Ruthless.

"It looks like you on another thirty pounds of muscle!" said Tricky. Ruthless was looking at all the extracurricular activities going on. There was a time when Ruthless would get a rush from the boulevard from getting into brawls with those rivals from Brady Tucker to enjoying the nightlife smoking Dungeon Dragons and drinking Overcast Malt liquor, but for some reason, Ruthless felt like there was a new individual trying to reach the surface.

Ruthless was striving to become a MOE, which is known as a man of enlightenment. He also knew that there were some bridges he had to cross in order to get to his final destination. The first bridge was to apologize to Rebecca for what he did to her many Foolish Fridays ago.

Stan Goldstein was letting himself indulge on his favorite night crawler. Susan didn't have enough money to pay Stan to take her brother's case. So Stan made a simple request for Susan to prove to him that his case was worth taking. When Susan was finished giving Stan the ride of his life, he simply accepted the case and gave her a get-out-of-trouble card so he can cash in again. Then Stan made it clear that if he got her brother from going to B-Have County, she must get him off for a week. Susan just licked her lips as she picked up her clothes and made her way to the bathroom. Stan got dressed, left $200 on the dresser, and then left the hotel.

While Stan was walking to his car, he had no idea Ms. Bradshaw and PS were watching his every move. Ms. Bradshaw just shook her head and said to herself, "His wife must be real smart or real stupid!"

PS explained to Ms. Bradshaw that Mrs. Goldstein understood that in order to become victorious, you must play by the rules and have a great strategy. About ten minutes later, Susan got in the car and gave Ms. Bradshaw the $200 and PS the Double Z chip that recorded her becoming one with Mr. Goldstein. PS then gave Susan $10,000 in a yellow envelope. PS signaled to Susan to exit the car, and then he whispered in her ear that if she stays loyal to the strategy, all her problems would be taken care of. Susan began to take off her clothes right in front of PS and told him that he could put his strategy on her anytime. Ms. Bradshaw gave Susan a look like if she didn't leave, the only thing she was going to see was the early morning yellow moonshine.

CHAPTER

12

Brad was happy to be out of the hospital. Brad was in a kind daze for lack of sleep. Coach looked at Brad and knew he could not send him back to D'Ville Campus after everything that transpired these past couple of days. First thing Coach did was inform Brad's parents, but the hard part was informing the team. Coach knew how much everybody on the team loved Brad and how shaken up the team was to see him have a meltdown, everyone except John.

All of a sudden, Brad just started saying, "Take flight. Take flight. Beware of the night. The moon is out, so guard your life!" Coach looked at the special sleeping pills Brad was prescribed to take as soon as they got home. Coach took it as a sign that it was time to have that conversation with the Master of The Universe.

It was Saturday night in D'Ville, and Club Blackout was expecting a big turnout. The multiplatinum hip-hop artist BP3 was performing live. Derrick, Smoove, and Spiff were escorted to the side door entrance. Once they were seated in the VIP booth, Smoove called the waitress over. On the other side of the club, Tricky, Ruthless, and Showdown were watching Derrick, Smoove, and Spiff.

Tricky never liked Derrick, especially when Derrick beat Tricky in the D'Ville High School championship. Rumor has it that Tricky was ineligible because of his grades, but it was his age that exposed him.

Tricky was just as good or even better than Derrick, but Tricky was tired of the politics holding him back. That was when he decided Trans Motor Boulevard and the ignorance of the people of the night would be his way of survival.

Spiff noticed the looks they were getting and had a silent conversation with J. Boogie to protect them. Showdown noticed that Spiff had his head down. He started laughing and nudged Ruthless and Tricky to take notice. Tricky also laughed, but Ruthless did not find anything funny about Spiff's actions.

Derrick kicked Spiff and told him to get a grip with the day walker stuff. "Man, you drawing too much attention on us, Spiff! Just be cool and enjoy the night!" stated Smoove. Spiff knew in his heart what he did was right, but he decided to take a backseat to J. Boogie and follow the energy of the night.

All of a sudden, all the lights in the club went out. Flashing red, white, and black lights started flashing across the stage. Then the DJ told the club to stand up and release the beast. The whole club erupted when BP3 came on stage. Then BP3 said to the crowd, "If you're a monster, make some noise! If you're a gorilla, make some noise. If you're a beast, make some more noise!" As for me, the crowd was jumping up and down, buzzing with anticipation for BP3 to say his opening lines to his famous single.

Then BP3 said, "I'm a monster, I'm a gorilla, I'm a beast! You better B-Have when you enter my county!" Everybody in the club went bonkers. The energy flowing through was at an all-time high. Derrick was looking directly at Tricky while BP3 was performing. PS was watching from his private booth all the events that were going on and feeding of the energy of the Club Blackout.

At midlevel, MD 20/20 and his shadows were standing across J. Boogie and his GL's. The atmosphere was intense. Both sides were ready to engage in an all-out brawl, as both sides felt they had total control of the fate of D'Ville. Everyone became real silent when the higher council of day and night made their appearance. MD 20/20 and J. Boogie approached the higher council with their enlightenment count. After reviewing both counts, the higher council stated, "Thanks to the actions of Nurse Rebecca and Dr. Richardson. The actions of MD20/20 and his shadows have been justified. However, due to the fact that Nurse Rebecca's grandmother is a devoted day walker, Nurse Rebecca is eligible to enter the skies above and have an opportunity to become a GL!" All the GL's began to rejoice and started singing, which pushed all of MD 20/20's shadows at least five hundred feet below midlevel.

MD 20/20 gave J. Boogie a smirk to let him know that this battle was only the beginning before he joined his shadows. J. Boogie knew MD 20/20 meant what he said. Then as he returned to the skies above, he understood why the Master of The Universe didn't get involved when Nurse Rebecca was being attack. It was all part of the master plan to obtain the unanimous decision.

CHAPTER

13

As Coach Kelly approached the hospital, he couldn't believe how ill Brad looked. Brad looked like he didn't sleep in at least five days, but he was only hospitalized for two. A tear strolled down Coach Kelly's face when he noticed how frail Brad had become. In two days, Brad went from weighing 220 lbs. to 170 lbs. The doctors explained to Coach that Brad would only drink grape juice, but he wouldn't eat or sleep.

The doctors also gave Coach Kelly some WND Pills to increase Brad's appetite. After gathering all this newfound information, Coach Kelly helped Brad to his car, and then they were on their way to Coach Kelly's house.

While Shavon was trying to figure out why Derrick gave her the cold shoulder while they saw each other at the diner, she began to fantasize about the day she will relocate to Sunshine Estates. She always saw herself living in a mansion with at least eight rooms like her grandparents did. Shavon's grandfather went off to D'Ville to make a name for himself. He felt in order to really get a true appreciation of the day, you must endure the test of the night. So at the age of sixteen, Shavon's grandfather went to D'Ville so he could become one with the Master of The Universe and get a better understanding of *The Strategy*.

John was thinking about how he could find a way to make Brad believe that what he saw was not real. As John finished reading page 285 of *The Strategy,* he felt an unusual but stimulating force flow through him. The last time he felt this energy was when he was standing in front of Shavon on Foolish Friday. John craved this feeling, and he knew that he had to have Shavon by any means necessary.

Back at Club Blackout, PS was sitting behind his desk counting all the profits he made on Foolish Friday—from the drinks at the bar, the Foolish Friday entrance fee, plus the special night crawler services. Now body-jumping, as they call it in D'Ville, was illegal, but when you got most of the police department on your payroll, who was going to stop you?

PS noticed three individuals looking to end BP3's performance earlier than expected when one of the individuals was making his way toward Derrick, Smoove, and Spiff. As Tricky was making his way to the VIP section, out of nowhere, a three-hundred-pound bouncer grabbed him from behind. The bouncer hit a secret button on the floor, and within seconds, they were in PS's office.

Tricky couldn't believe how fast he went from being in the club to being in an office. PS entered the office with a drink in his hand. Then he placed the glass in front of Tricky and said, "If you wanted a taste of Redemption, all you got to do is ask." Tricky took the glass and drank what he thought was the wine Redemption. Then PS said in a smooth, sinister voice, "Now enjoy the night!"

All of a sudden, Tricky was standing on stage butt naked humping the floor, screaming, "I'm a monster, I'm a gorilla, I'm a beast." Then PS called Sergeant Lang and told him he had another bug that needed to become exterminated. Tricky had been escorted out of the club in handcuffs. After watching what just took place, Spiff and Ruthless both knew something strange was looming in Club Blackout. They just couldn't put their finger on it.

PS was watching Ruthless's every move. He knew Ruthless Brad smart as well as dangerous, especially when it came to spotting the smoke screen. When Ruthless was just fifteen years old, PS took Ruthless under his wing and taught him everything he needed to know on the art of deception. What Ruthless didn't know back then was PS was also using him as bait.

Just as PS was about to switch the monitor to camera number 8, Stan Goldstein came dashing in pacing back and forth as if he had just seen a ghost. When PS saw the look of fear in his lawyer and so-called partner's face, he knew this was serious. "Something must be done about that, that so-called monster, gorilla, beast!" yelled Stan Goldstein. PS raised his eyebrow and looked over at Ms. Bradshaw to ensure her that he knew what Stan was about to reveal to them.

Stan went over to the ETV player and inserted the MP disc. All three watched the monitor, waiting to see what was going to appear on the sixty-four-inch screen. As the screen became clear, there was Mrs. Goldstein in Stan's office wearing nothing but a see-through white blouse. She bent over the desk and asked BP3 to give her the beast.

Mrs. Goldstein looked right into the screen as if she knew someone was watching. Then she winked and blew a kiss while BP3 was giving her the beast. For that split second, Ms. Bradshaw felt sorry for Mr. Goldstein, and then she caught herself and began plotting her next move on how to get the money.

When the escapade was over, BP3 signed a note and placed it on Mrs. Goldstein's lower back. The note read, "Good as Goldstein. Great representation!" PS looked at his lawyer's face and began to laugh on the inside. Stan felt hurt, humiliated, and powerless at the same time.

Then PS asked Stan, "Do you have a prenup?" Stan answered no. Then PS asked, "How did your wife have access to your secret office where you take your female clients?" Stan felt stupid when PS asked that question because that's where he paid Ms. Bradshaw and made a pass at her. PS knew that he had his so-called partner at his mercy. Now PS looked Stan right in the eye and told him, "I see what I can do!" Stan shook PS's hand and left his office, feeling satisfied. Ms. Bradshaw walked over to the ETV player and noticed Stan forgot his MP disc. Right on cue, PS told Ms. Bradshaw to keep it and receive double for her troubles.

It was the first Sunday after the day walker revival. People were making their way inside the lighthouse. Spiff couldn't stop thinking about what took place at Club Blackout last night. That whole night, he couldn't shake off this unusual but enticing vibe going through the club. He couldn't relax because he was afraid what Ruthless was going to say if he truly was trying to become a day walker. Spiff thought to himself, *I got as much leverage on him as he got on me because everyone is just waiting to see if he is just a night crawler in hiding!* Spiff felt his ultimate being warn him that he was stepping out of sight.

Spiff entered the lighthouse, closed his eyes, and had a private conversation with the Master of The Universe. When Spiff opened his eyes, he noticed Ruthless sitting right in front of him, and sitting across him was Shavon and John Goldstein.

The clock showed that it was 10:00 am, but the sky was pitch-black. As Derrick stared out the window, he couldn't help but notice Ms. Bradshaw walked seductively across D'Ville St. Campus. As if she knew that someone was watching, Ms. Bradshaw bent over in slow motion to show off all her assets. Ms. Bradshaw stood up, turned around, and blew a kiss at Derrick who couldn't take his eyes off her.

All of a sudden, Derrick heard a loud knock at the door. Derrick was hoping it was Shavon coming over to become one with each other, but when he opened the door, it was Smoove. Derrick could see that Smoove was feeling real good about himself, especially since he started getting the money.

"What's going on in Mr. Rodgers's neighborhood?" Derrick asked.

"Ah, it feels good to get some money! You know what I mean?" stated Smoove.

Derrick just sat there in silence. He was still amazed how everything just seemed to always go his way. Derrick wanted to warn Smoove that being one with Ms. Bradshaw was taking a serious risk, but he decided to just focus on his relationship dilemma.

It was twelve noon. The sky was as dark as it could be on this Sunday after Foolish Friday weekend. Shavon just lay in her bed contemplating if she should call Derrick. But something real deep inside her wanted to call John. Ever since their encounter the other night, Shavon could not stop thinking about John. Shavon knew she was swimming in shark-infested water if she got close to Derrick's main enemy. What Shavon felt from John's presence was intoxicating and powerful. And she loved every minute of it.

John just finished reading page 275 of *The Strategy*. While closing his eyes to see the unseen, John witnessed Shavon thinking about their last encounter. The deeper he tried to look, the harder it was to see. John always felt that Shavon was wasting her time with Derrick. John felt that Shavon was from a different world than Derrick, a world that Derrick could never understand. All of a sudden, John heard this deep and creepy voice call his name. John immediately opened his eyes just to see a shadow of himself. The voice whispered, "If you reach for it, you can have it! Stay focused and confuse your enemies!" John began to meditate on those words. There was so much he wanted, and he knew what he had to do to get it.

Later that afternoon, Derrick got a phone call from Coach Kelly. At first, Derrick thought about not answering it, but his inner being urged him to take the call. When Derrick heard the fear in Coach Kelly's voice, he knew it was something that will affect the team. Coach simply said to come to the team film room in five minutes. Then he hung up the phone.

Derrick's mind was racing. He wondered what could have happened that got Coach so rattled. Then Derrick's phone rang again. It was Shavon. Derrick answered. Derrick waited for Shavon to speak, but she didn't say a word. Then she hung up. Derrick just shrugged and headed for the team film room.

When Derrick reached the entrance, he was greeted by Spiff, Smoove, and John. Derrick didn't know what to make of the encounter, but when he saw Smoove and Spiff crying, he knew it wasn't good. When Coach saw that Derrick had arrived, he told him to come inside the team film room. Derrick walked in the team film room just to notice the DVD and TV were set, and Brad's Jersey was draped across his chair. Derrick already knew where this was going. Coach turned on the DVD and let Derrick watch the horrible footage. Derrick's heart just jumped out of his chest. Derrick just broke down and cried. He couldn't believe that Brad would take himself out like that.

It was too much for Derrick to handle. Derrick picked up a chair and threw it at the television. Coach felt Derrick's pain and understood his actions. Then the rest of the team came in to try to calm down Derrick—everyone except John.

Trans Motor Boulevard was buzzing with excitement. The night crawlers were out, the moon was glowing, and BP3 was on the boulevard enjoying the street festival better known as boulevard block party. Tricky and Showdown was also enjoying the party, especially all the money they making tonight. Tricky also seemed to be getting a little more attention than usual these days. Every time he walked around D'Ville, people would say, "Here is the monster, the gorilla, the beast!"

Showdown could not stop laughing after seeing his partner make a fool of himself at the BP3 performance at the club. Tricky used it to his advantage by performing private parties for some of the most powerful women in D'Ville and getting to become one with them also.

BP3 was enjoying himself a little too much at the boulevard block party. Women kept walking up to him, grabbing his manhood, making reference to give them the beast. BP3 began to unzip his five-star jeans and then stopped when he saw PS pulled up. PS look at Tricky and Showdown and then gave Showdown the signal to put an end to all the fun and games that was running Mr. Sanders's business.

Tricky couldn't wait to approach BP3 and show him how a real monster handles his business. Just as Tricky was about to pull out his GX-54 Shooter, Ruthless walked on Tricky and told him that he was being set up, and D'Ville Police was watching him from two blocks away. As Tricky got closer, not paying attention to his friend's warning, Tricky pulled out his gun. BP3 stared right down the barrel of his GX-54 Shooter. The D'Ville Police began to rush Tricky. Then Ruthless closed his eyes and had a private conversation with J. Boogie. Ruthless didn't want to see his friend and partner in numerous crimes get sent to B-Have County or worse. When Ruthless opened his eyes, he noticed everyone was gone—everyone except the D'Ville Police and Showdown.

Shavon decided to do a little spring cleaning when she got up this morning. She felt that is was time to put the past behind her if she were ever going to move forward. Amy just sat there and watched her cousin throw all of Derrick's clothes and his other important items away in a box that had the words "waste of time" written on it. Amy wanted to say something but felt it was best to stay out of it.

On the other side of campus, Derrick decided to close himself off to everyone this Sunday. Just the thought of Brad killing himself was just too much for him to handle. He noticed he had twenty text messages and four voicemails since he stormed out of the team film room. Too many thoughts started to race through his mind. This whole day walker, night crawler stuff just didn't make any sense. So Derrick decided to smoke an unlimited amount of Dungeon Dragons, sip on some Redemption, and enjoy the nightlife.

Spiff did what he usually does on Sunday, which was go to the lighthouse to listen to Finder O'Johnson give his guiding light of the day. Spiff decided to call Derrick, but when his G-phone went straight to voicemail, he decided not to leave a message. Spiff felt a little heavyhearted after hearing about Brad taking his own life. Spiff knew the Master of The Universe will make sense of everything that transpired in his universe.

Spiff knocked over a book that was lying on his nightstand. When he picked it up, he noticed it was a collection of his poems, goals, and pictures of his D'Ville games. Spiff was flipping through the pages when he came across a poem that caught his eye. It was titled "Five as One." The poem read:

One of us could shoot,
One of us can't!
One of us is a beast when the crowd chants!
One of us holds down the middle and finish.
One of us makes all of us look Smoove.
Five as one. And I cannot forget about teammate number 6
Who goes by the name of Spiff!
Just me and my teammates that I consider my family.
Always sunny when I'm chilling with my boys in D'Ville!

Spiff just shed a tear after reading Brad's poem. Brad gave it to him when he went to the day walker make it do what it do day. Brad told Spiff not to open it until after they win a championship or their last game as D'Ville St. players.

Finder O'Johnson was putting the finishing touches to the guiding light of the day. He was going to explain to his following elevators that they originated from overachievers, and they were not to accept being referred to as bottom feeders, night crawlers, or people of the night. Finder O'Johnson had to pause and think about how the Master of The Universe had allowed him to remove his shades twenty-five years ago. He knew in his inner being that he needed to go on the journey of elevation if he was going to escape the burn of the sizzle.

Before Finder O'Johnson said yes to his journey, the sizzle would give him such a rush to do any and everything that brought him pleasure. That lifestyle was hard to walk away from on his own will because that burn could still creep up inside your inner being and take control over you even if you are a day walker.

Once you get the sizzle, it becomes a part of you. Finder O'Johnson witnessed too many people die in his inner circle from the sizzle. Not one person knew how many cool-down treatments and fluid sessions he must do in order to stay healthy. Finder O'Johnson just looked up at the sky, put one finger in the air, and said, "Thanks to the Master of The Universe for being the guiding light to a city surrounded by darkness."

Then out of nowhere, Spiff walked into Finder O'Johnson's office because he was disturbed about what happened to Brad. After reading Brad's poem, Spiff needed a flashlight on the situation. Finder O'Johnson read the poem, paused, looked at Spiff, and told him that he might want to sit down before he gives him the flashlight of this tragic situation.

Derrick was still in a state of shock. He just couldn't understand why Brad would just take his life like that. Brad always seemed upbeat and positive about everyone and everything. Derrick thought that it was kind of strange and naive to ignore the negative side of life, but that's what made Brad such a cool person to be around.

All of a sudden, Derrick heard a knock at the door. Derrick decided not to answer it, but when he saw who was on the other side, he couldn't let her walk away. Derrick opened the door, and Shavon embraced him with such a passionate kiss. Derrick couldn't contain himself and picked up Shavon and carried her to his bed. Derrick liked every inch of her body from head to toe. Shavon just closed her eyes while Derrick was taking her to paradise. They continued to become one with each other, and then out of nowhere, Shavon got up, put on her clothes, and walked out without even saying a word. Derrick tried to pull Shavon back into his room, but Shavon resisted and smacked Derrick's hand. Shavon looked right into Derrick's eyes and said, "There is good people and people who has a strategy! Which one are you?"

Derrick's mind went blank and did not understand what Shavon meant by that statement. As Shavon continued to leave Derrick's room, she decided to meet up with John. Shavon felt something from their last encounter, and she wanted to feel it again. Maybe on a deeper level.

Sergeant Lang was giving his exterminators their assignments of the day. They knew things would be a little slow today being that Foolish Friday and Shutdown Saturday has come and went. Sergeant Lang was not happy with the low B-Have County count. He couldn't put his finger on it. Neither could the upper ranks of the D'Ville Police put their fingers on it either. Sergeant Lang thought to himself, *Maybe it is time to turn up the heat of the street!*

CHAPTER

15

Just as Sergeant Lang was leaving the upper ranks office, PS was standing in front of his car. Before Sergeant Lang could speak, PS handed him an envelope that gave him the answer to his low B-Have County count. Sergeant Lang opened up envelope, looked inside of it, and knew the individual right off the back. The man was no other than Zerega Hill. But in D'Ville, he was known as the legendary source Little Man Z. PS and Sergeant Lang looked at each other, and then they went their separate ways to put their plan in motion—the setup of Little Man Z, the increase of the B-Have snatch-up count, and PS having to complete control of the night.

Back in the skies above, there was a GL meeting with J. Boogie. The GL's were ready for their assignments as the battle against MD 20/20, and his shadows was getting near. GL 54 was very anxious to go to battle, especially after what happened to Brad—thanks to the actions of MD 20/20. GL 54 warned J. Boogie about letting Brad become friends with John, but J. Boogie told GL 54 that the Master of The Universe controls every action, and we must *follow his actions before we take action.*

When GL 54 saw Brad being attacked at the championship game, he wanted to take action, but J. Boogie gave him the beam stare and told him, "Stand down. Stand down! This is part of the master plan!" GL 54 was hoping this meeting was about taking action with aggressive force. The horn sounded, and the Master of The Universe and J. Boogie entered the inner circle. All the GL's took one knee and acknowledged them with one finger up and heads down.

The Master of The Universe told the GL's to rise and pay attention to the message of J. Boogie. J. Boogie felt an unusual presence coming from the crowd of GL's. J. Boogie gave his assignments and noticed that MD 20/20, disguised as an GL, was whispering inside of GL 54's inner ear. The Master of The Universe smiled and gave J. Boogie a signal to continue as if he didn't see MD 20/20.

Before J. Boogie could finish, GL 54 stood up and blamed J. Boogie's lack of leadership as the main reason behind Brad's death. Just when J. Boogie was about to strike him, the Master of The Universe said, "If that's is how you feel, you can turn in your top flight and go down to midlevel." GL 54 thought about it long and hard, but the influence of MD 20/20 had overtaken him. So he finally decided to fly solo and go down to midlevel. J. Boogie told him that he was entering the point of no return and once he rejected his membership. GL 54 said to J. Boogie, "I was never a member! Just playing my position for something greater!" GL's 54 words wounded J. Boogie, but he knew that the battle for D'Ville would cause conflict if he stayed.

CHAPTER

16

Derrick thought about paying Shavon an unexpected visit, but as he was about to leave his apartment, his phone ranged. It was an unusual number that appeared. Derrick didn't answer it, but this unusual number kept calling him back. Finally, after the six time, he answered it. A stunned look came across his face when he heard who was on the other end of the phone. The voice said, "I know the pain you are feeling, and I also know the look of confusion you have on your face right now! I can take away your pain and give you some clarity, plus some other incentives!"

Just as the person hung up the phone, Smoove and Spiff came barging in to tell Derrick that they saw Shavon leaving John's house not too long ago. Derrick just gave a blank stare out of his window and just plopped down on his bed as if he didn't hear what Smoove and Spiff just said. Smoove turned around to notice that Spiff was no longer there.

Back at the lighthouse, Finder O'Johnson just put the flashlight to Brad's poem. Spiff eagerly waited for Finder O'Johnson to explain the meaning of the poem. While Finder O'Johnson was about to speak, he began to start sweating, and then he asked Spiff, "Do you know how good it feels to become one with a stranger?" Spiff always knew there was something strange about Finder O'Johnson, and now it was starting to be revealed. Behind these strange and weird antics of Finder O'Johnson were the works of MD 20/20 and his shadows.

J. Boogie was puzzled by the betrayal of GL 54. All of a sudden, a code red went through the skies above. J. Boogie saw that Finder O'Johnson was under attack and was left unguarded—thanks to the actions of GL 54. So in a blink of an eye, J. Boogie came to Finder O'Johnson's rescue and took out the shadows and watched MD 20/20 flee. Just as Finder O'Johnson was coming back to his senses, he could see that Spiff was looking and judging how this man was able to lead us through this state of darkness when he hadn't shine the light in his own affairs. Spiff took the poem and decided not to stay for the guiding light of the day. He felt he needed to do some investigating of his own about Finder O'Johnson and what he was hiding.

On Trans Motor Boulevard, Tricky and Showdown decided to go through with the plan to take BP3 out of his misery. Stan Goldstein gave his clients the propulsion to kidnap and kill the so-called Rapper. Little did Stan know that PS doubled what Stan paid Tricky and Showdown to carry out a different mission.

Stan met with Tricky on the corners of Trans Motor Boulevard and Three Hundred Ninth Street. Sergeant Lang was watching from two blocks, hoping he could get what he was looking for. Stan got in the car and asked, "Is the job taken care of, guys?"

Showdown smacked Stan in the back of the head and told him, "Keep cool! We going to the secret location said Tricky."

As the car stopped at the red light, Stan heard banging coming from the trunk. Stan started smiling to himself as he thought about the look on BP3's face when Tricky and Showdown finished what he started. *Money well spent,* Stan thought to himself. Finally, the car came to a stop. Tricky handed Stan a blindfold and told him to put it on. Stan thought Tricky was playing, but when Showdown pulled out his GTF Super 6 gun and put it in his gut, Stan just played by the rules and laughed when he visualized Tricky and Showdown beating the living hell out of BP3.

As Tricky and Showdown walked Stan into the dark alley, he heard all sorts of unusual sounds and smells coming from the alley. There were bottom feeders and night crawlers everywhere. The bottom feeders were waiting for Stan so they could rip him off. As Stan was told to stop and take off his blindfold, he couldn't believe what he was seeing. His wife, Mrs. Goldstein, was standing side by side with BP3, Tricky, Showdown, Ms. Bradshaw, and PS. Stan was standing there looking speechless. Stan knew that his day has finally caught up with him. First, the bottom feeders stripped him down of his suit, money, possessions, and ID. Then Tricky, Showdown, and Ms. Bradshaw tied him up to a chair in front of a TV and turned on the large eighty-inch screen. Stan couldn't believe what he was watching. He had no idea he was caught red-handed trying to make a secret deal to buy out PS from owning the D'Ville Deceptions.

Stan tried to explain himself, but Showdown punched him so hard in his gut. Stan threw up right on the spot. PS and Sergeant Lang entered the alley. Stan was filled with fear when he saw PS's eyes turn black. PS could smell his fear and enjoyed the fragrance. PS asked Stan, "Do you really think you can be the king?" Before Stan could speak, PS sliced his cheek slowly so Stan could feel every inch of pain. As the blood began to drip slowly down his face, PS's heart began to beat one hundred times a minute. Everyone could see PS was enjoying every moment of this. Then PS gave Ms. Bradshaw a slip on MG Razor and told her to give Stan the ride of his *life*.

Everyone in the alley felt sorry for Stan, but in a sick-twisted kind of way, they wish they could become one with Ms. Bradshaw. Ms. Bradshaw took off her clothes, and then she put on the MG Razor slip. Stan got so excited that he forgot about the hidden razor that was about to make contact with his manhood. Ms. Bradshaw gave him a kiss and whispered in his ear, "Let me take you to heaven." Stan could no longer contain himself as he told her to put his key into her lock and turn it.

As Ms. Bradshaw put Stan's manhood inside her, he felt something sharp gliding against his manhood. Ms. Bradshaw began to grind faster and faster. Stan started screaming in pain as the MG Razor kept going up and down against his manhood. Stan asked Ms. Bradshaw if she could please stop, but she said, "Baby, I'm about to take you to heaven!

Ohh, I'm almost there." Tricky and Showdown both felt sorry for Stan, but they also had to get paid.

After Ms. Bradshaw climaxed, she slowly got up from Stan's lap. Then she let out a devilish smirk and said, "Damn, baby! Your loving is as good as Goldstein. When all the men saw how slashed up Stan's manhood was, they all walked out, grabbing their lower region and were no longer attracted to Ms. Bloody Bradshaw. Stan was going into shock and begged PS to stop, and he was sorry for double-crossing him.

PS, with a sinister laugh, said, "You tried to screw me. I'm just giving you what you truly wanted all along." PS then began to pour honey barbecue sauce all over Stan. Then he told Tricky and Showdown to release the hounds. Everyone in the ally vanished because PS's hounds loved the sight, smell, and taste of blood.

As BP3 and Mrs. Goldstein came into the alley with the hounds, both of them started laughing hysterically when they saw how defeated Stan looked. As Monique left the alley, she locked eyes with Mrs. Goldstein and couldn't believe how she could set up her own husband like that. Monique began to cry and feel sorry for all the pain and agony Stan was in as the hounds teared him apart. PS handed an envelope to Mrs. Goldstein containing $2 million. In return, she gave PS all the documents to his business that she signed over to him.

When BP3 and Mrs. Goldstein drove off, PS asked Sergeant Lang id he did get all the video evidence he needed. Sergeant Lang said he got everything he needed. Then PS gave Sergeant Lang their secret handshake.

"Looks like somebody is going to B-Have County!" said PS.

Then Sergeant Lang agreed and said, "Yeah, a monster, a gorilla, and a beast!" They both left Stan's lifeless body in the alley to send a message that you don't cross the boss.

17

Back at the lighthouse, the crowd was getting a little anxious as they noticed that it was almost 9:30 a.m., and there was no sign of Finder O'Johnson. Spiff couldn't help but have a little smirk come across his face. Deep down, Spiff wanted the lighthouse to see that Finder O'Johnson was just another man who was not who he claimed to be. He was just another human struggling to overcome the work of the dark.

"The Path of Jealousy is like taking a stroll with a deceptive lover!" J. Boogie said to Spiff's inner being. Then all of a sudden, Finder O'Johnson made his way into the lighthouse and told the crowd that they had a guest speaker who was ready to join forces in this battle against the people of the night. The guest speaker was Zerega Hill, a.k.a. Little Man Z. The crowd was speechless. They all heard of the stories how he got rid of the Dirtbag Empire in Paradise Place and how he reclaimed Focus City from the hands of the Swine Sinister Crew.

Everyone stood up and cheered for Little Man Z—everyone except John Goldstein who had his own reasons for being in the lighthouse.

Back at the ground below, MD 20/20 was happy with how his plans were unfolding. He knew the Master of The Universe was going to bring Little Man Z back into the game, but he had a surprise attack on how he was going to win that battle. With Finder O'Johnson starting to feel the sizzle and GL 54 becoming a shadow, MD 20/20 was feeling pretty good about his next move. He was already proud of his shadows for their influence of the murder of Stan Goldstein, but more death, destruction, and deception was to come—thanks to MD 20/20's love of bloodshed and one step closer for him to try to gain total control of the universe.

Derrick was still trying to put all the pieces together—Shavon acting strange, Brad being killed, Ms. Bradshaw playing him close while being one with Smoove. It just wasn't making any sense to him, just too much confusion happing all at one time. Derrick wanted to call Spiff but didn't want him to get all deep on him. Finally, Derrick decided to go to Club Blackout. He thought that if he gave PS back the $50,000, then all this unexpected drama would leave his surroundings.

As Derrick approached the side door to the club, he noticed that someone was watching him. He turned around, but there was no one there. Then out of nowhere, a real dark and eerie voice said, "I'm going to destroy you the same way I destroyed your father!" When Derrick heard what the voice had said, he picked up a bat that had just happened to be in the street at that time and started swinging like he was a power hitter for the D'Ville Baseball Team on the black GTX Turbo 300. Derrick kept swinging and swinging until his arms got real bloody and tired. When he dropped the bat, he noticed Sergeant Lang, PS, and Shavon watching Derrick in disbelief. Sergeant Lang said to Derrick, "For that stunt, looks like someone needs to learn how to B-Have." As Sergeant Lang handcuffed Derrick and put him in the back of the D'Ville police car, he whispered to him that his dad would have been so proud of him. Derrick began to cry because he knew that one day, his emotions were going to get the best of him, and it did *big time.*

"Let's on, showgirls!" yelled the in-your-place guard. The bright light burned Derrick's eyes so bad he had to close them. When the guard saw Derrick closed his eyes, he pulled out his day switch and pressed it. Derrick never felt such a sharp pain go through his brain. He opened his eyes instantly and begged the guard to stop. The guard said, "You is lucky Sergeant Lang is watching because the next time you close your eyes will be your last, showgirl!" Then the bright lights dimmed a little as Derrick was being escorted into B-Have County.

Spiff couldn't sleep. He was calling Derrick's room and his cell phone and didn't get a response. So Spiff called Nathan, but when Nathan's phone went straight to voicemail, he began to feel real uneasy. So he decided to spend some one-on-one time with *The Good Book* and see where the Master of The Universe would lead him. Spiff opened to the middle of the book and stopped on page J-221. It read, "Don't be troubled by the things that can't be seen for through confusion will produce clarity." Spiff was still confused, but an overwhelming feeling of peace and relaxation entered his inner being. He fell into a deep sleep and knew that his friend was in good hands.

"OK, SHOWGIRLS. TIME TO GET SOME SHUT-EYE!" yelled Pit Guard Turner. He also explained that in B-Have County, you must put on your bright light patches during shut-eye because for the next sixteen hours, the light is gonna be set to one thousand multivolts. If a person opens his eyes without wearing their bright light patches, he could suffer severe brain trauma and double vision. Derrick remembered how his eyes felt earlier, and he was not trying to have another bad experience. Now everyone prepared themselves for shut-eye, but there was one individual who didn't wear any bright light patches. It was like he was accustomed to the burning one thousand multivolts.

He just sat there, eyes closed, sitting Indian-style, not moving a single muscle. Then Pit Guard Tuner yelled, "OK, Bridge, that's enough with that accepting THE TRUTH SHIT!" Bridge just got up, went straight to his bed—eyes closed—and went straight to sleep.

When Pit Guard Turner left, all the B-Havior population was chanting: "Bridge is *the truth*. Bridge is *the truth*. If you wanna know, you must *pay the toll!*"

Derrick never witnessed that kind of power from any individual. It was a different kind of power, not the kind that is used through fear. It was like Bridge had this untapped energy flowing stronger than the one-thousand-multivolt lights. Little did Derrick know Bridge was able to feel his ultra being. It was just a matter of time before Derrick would cross *the bridge*.

CHAPTER

18

In the skies above, J. Boogie was pacing back and forth. The Master of The Universe saw the confused look on his face. The Master of The Universe, in a calm voice, said, "My son, don't worry! We will win in the end!"

Before J. Boogie could respond, he noticed that MD 20/20 was standing to his left. J. Boogie wanted to attack him on sight, but the Master of The Universe raised his right hand, giving the signal for J. Boogie to be still. MD 20/20, as arrogant as he can be, approached the Master of The Universe and spit on J. Boogie's foot in the process.

Before MD 20/20 could speak, J. Boogie had his hand around his slimy neck. MD 20/20 slipped out and just laughed. The master raised his thunderous voice, and everyone stopped dead in their tracks. Then the Master of The Universe told MD 20/20 that he had five minutes before he get sent back to the world below.

MD 20/20 said, "It's just a matter of time before I have total control of D'Ville, and then I'm coming for your *head!* Oh, and, J. Boogie, I will make you my personal assistant, if you know what I mean!"

The Master of The Universe got up from his throne, kicked MD 20/20 in the gut, then picked him up with three fingers, and threw him back down to the world below. The GL's cleaned up the foul-smelling green liquid that MD 20/20 spit up after he was kicked. The master sat back on his throne and gave J. Boogie the order to go down to D'Ville and protect the citizens from the day walkers, the truth dealers, the night crawlers, and the bottom feeders from the outer-body experience of MD 20/20 and his shadows. Then the master said, "Remember, son, those who submit themselves to the Master of The Universe. Resist MD 20/20, and he will flee from them! Also, they will know you as the one and only commissioner of the universe."

Derrick woke up and received a note. The note was sitting next to his bed. The note read, "Be sober minded. Be watchful. Your adversary MD 20/20 prowls around like a roaring lion, seeking someone to devour. Resist him, stay firm in your faith (1 Peter 5:8–9)."

Derrick knew who sent the note but didn't understand why. Then all of a sudden, Sergeant Lang told Derrick he was free, and he could go back to D'Ville. Derrick put the note in his pocket, left with Sergeant Lang, and prepared himself going back to D'Ville and dealing with the people of the night.

Then Derrick noticed another note, and it read, "Also remember, Derrick, anyone who believes and is baptized will be saved. But anyone who refuses to believe will be condemned. These miraculous signs will accompany those who believe. They will cast out demons in my name and speak in new languages. They will be able to handle snakes with safety, and if they drink anything poisonous, it won't hurt them. They will be able to place their hands on the sick, and they will be healed. So you know what must be done! *Believe in the one and only Master of The Universe in the name of his son, the commissioner of the* (Mark 16:15–18). Stay strong and be humble! Your boy, Bridge." The Commissioner of Universe WHO's name is YHWHisWay! Y - Way for short and Not J. Boogie! Derrick. Time to Rise and Let your Light Shine! From your fellow Day Walker, Bridge.